SONG OF MARRIAGE

A Chronicle of Love, Life, Light, and Laughter

To Paul
We became
friends the
first time
we met on
the March 2005
at Hotel
Villaggio !
— Rajesh

SONG OF MARRIAGE

A Chronicle of Love, Life, Light and Laughter

Rajesh Dutta

ZORBA BOOKS

ZORBA BOOKS

Publishing Services in India by Zorba Books, 2019

Website: www.zorbabooks.com
Email: info@zorbabooks.com

Print Book ISBN 978-93-88497-45-9
E-book ISBN 978-93-88497-46-6

Zorba Books Pvt. Ltd.(opc)
Gurgaon, INDIA

Printed in India

To us four because we were always there

About the author

The author is a little bit of sunlight in the depths of much older winters. His life is the summer camp of school kids. He serves life's purposes by trying very hard to be himself at home and as a teacher of English in a school in Gurgaon. He has not yet reached that stage where you could say he now belongs to the society of old hiking leaves of autumn. He switches off the lights at 11.30 pm and is groggily back into the light at an unearthly hour in order to create the twenty fifth hour for writing. He left the joggers long ago and he is now finding that gaining weight is a lot easier. He believes that cooking food is a way to becoming more useful around the house besides balcony-gardening, massaging heads and feet and egos.

Also by the author:

Death of a Robin
Second Robin

If the record of the universe is right then nothing written in this book ever happened and memories certainly haven't been used at all. Any resemblance to any names of characters, people and places is also pure fiction.

I
Foundation

1.

A Paean

*M*edia wives welcome books written about them but I have taken a big risk in writing this one.

Picture among women a phenomenon called wife whose face finally a husband gets to understand over a period of time. Now picture among women an idea called Kaia and you can label her each day differently. Begin your tour with the head which may be anything any day, say for example, a temple; the face is an idol or idols with astrological makeup; the eyes altar strong, like moving candles. Within many stories in each feature, the trimmings of a magical mythology, everyday satisfy one's quest for a pantheon. Another day, she is a natural formation. The forehead is stable tableland, occasionally lit with the natural lights of the moors of piousness. Yet another day, it is nature itself. The ears rise and set behind a cloud of hair at the mercy of which I and the whole house are. Next, it's culture and civilisation. The cheeks are not at all a wide gallery but you can raise the culture of a city there. On delicate display is the nose, without extremes. Without inner shows. Within the context of commitment is the modest mouth, a rose at your service, always with a bit of something new in its reciprocal passionate kiss. Her tongue is a mistress to which the book of Ecclesiastes, chapter 3, verse 7 applies. A time to keep silence and a time to speak. Most words she speaks are like gracious brushing moments of sweet honey. Even her company invests in her voice. Her teeth are caged people when she is angry and when happy, a procession of characters going to attend an investiture ceremony. When she laughs, the interpretation changes without exposing long gums as is the case with perfect women. The neck is a sophisticated course of continuity from the chin from where you could crawl down to her heart.

A woman's compositions are a man's conquests but her heart takes prisoners. For two and a half decades, I have been one, comfortably lost in unaffordable rooms there. Talking about room, she is the last person to make any room even least crowded with her presence. Her arms are willowy extensions of the softest fairy woods of plural love. Humans can best be understood from how each of us wants death. I have envisaged my entry point into the tomb. It's her belly button, revealed in dignified freedom from the folds of the sari. The feet are her identity (in her own words, 'Peacocks have ugly feet'). Her fierceness reposes in them which has earned her the nickname *Latto*. That she does not take responsibility for their movement, is a testimony borne by the victims. She is approachable but likes to be attended to with excessive humor. There is no past with her. Every moment has to die. A new one has to take birth. Each gesture, without act or art, is a seed for many more unpredictable ones. A most natural mate for a man, she is submissive to nothing and no one except only, and I repeat, humor. While her sister, a prosperous postmodern lady, can make the most modern conversation, Kaia remains a conservative constant of talk. Never on the hard streets of coarse babble or forced verbalization or occasional lies, her management of politeness is nearly exemplary of the good lady, her sister, who also manages minds. Kaia is fixed with a moment monitor as her time is for work-use, in her prescribed roles as wife, mother and employee among many others.

Kaia is a metaphor for what's decent in this world. She is a compelling image of overwhelming emotion and classical shock when she encounters, unromantic thrill, wasted wasteful and waste of traditions, juggling Johns and Jennies, unspurred minds, death entertainers, flesh-proud Helens, unartistic death, death's features in any form, death in italics and not straight, clothing from nude stores, a face of hunger, friendless worlds, languages without voices, sun driven and forced to set, erotic buffalos, naked hair, shapeless husband, laughter rituals, panties on sale, alternatives to life, aniconic stars, landscaped women, male impurity, abusive night, cries of loss, gaps in fort, citizens of sin cities, sadness vacation, not knowing the surprise, part love, booked death, being short-hearted, setbacks at work, work-served beyond capacity, borrowed reflection, upside down people, momentary greatness, unimpaired wickedness, reeking fires, phallic anal and vaginal satires, all calamities, friction, literary vulnerability, mythical snacks, absence of apology, scorned apology, breast models, unused days, passive melting, un-consenting adults, one dollar shows and movies, manuals of sex, night consorts, being alone, end of dependence, traditions of the young, purposeless enemy, body liberties, postponed goodness, updated food from fridge, procreation out of love and marriage, primitive childhood, proud perfection, body series, sold love, ambiguities, illegal fondling, contrasting genitals, whatever's not time but passes, love difference, feel of falling or whitening hair, walking by luck, mother-sister-husband-children-directed world, exchange of offspring, loose love, love's Greek and Latin, virgin ways, a body in italics and not a straight one. And I could go on and on....

Her skin serves crystal drinks. The wine just does not erode. In fact, I have aged on the double whereas time only comes and sniffs at her. Years don't define her. Age doesn't confine her. She has a woman's body. A goddess's soul. She is a Leda in field attire. An Aphrodite without any. Her version of the female, with shapely breaks in its continuity, is an experience of the idolized beginnings or ends of Venus's naked roomfuls in which I am always a newlywed. She is such a bunch. Handfuls. Armfuls. Each encounter with her is a symphony of screaming music. In her empire of effeminacy, she completes, with conquering conditioners and honored perfumes, each ritual of womanhood like a queen. I have made my king's peace with Kaia's rule. I have to teach my literature to take a practiced step in her direction. She, who is already art, enters my imagination and sets up a new exhibition on the steamy streets of love every now and then. It is a silent fulfilment of two bodies understanding each other. I suffer from a genuine intoxication with the preservatives that soak her from the female thresholds, where makeup makes the rose, to the stoic depths of *her last foundation*. And that was when she was strongly recommended to be a wife.

And forthwith a husband hunt began.

2.
Manhunt

October 1992

My sleep is to be discerned from rest.

I was a laugh maker but I made some tears with laughter when they found me. The chief of the husband hunters, Wendy Peters, was the one. She aimed straight at my heart at the end of the Church service, of all the places and times. 'Die!' She said, 'Or make a home!' I thought she meant it for herself. 'Not available.' She looked me long in the eye. 'Don't be presumptuous! There are many your equal and some even better, so no, certainly not with me!' She had a lynched-mouth expression 'Come here!' and taking me aside with only a table between us, she asked me to sit. The air hardened between us. 'What is your age?' I had secrets but age? I told her. Next, she asked, 'What are your marriage plans?' At this, my intelligence which had hitherto separated itself from me returned and I stopped laughing. 'There is a girl whose parents are looking for a match. Are you interested?' I was not an artist of conversation but with thin films of self-condemnation, guilt, etc. I managed to make the right faces at her. Reading my look's turned pages, she said, 'I don't mind the feuds we have. I know you think my family is from some politico-religious zoo but we are people too.' I appealed 'Please forgive me. I have been very brutal. I have served darkness...' She interrupted 'Well, this is your opportunity now to save yourself, to get some light in your life by getting a wife in your life. Now give me a number where I can reach you this evening.' She engaged further. 'Consider this as the church coming to you in spite of what all you think of it. Let this be a teaching.' The world became a wonder of life and I gave her the number of my landlord.

I found the heart of nature on my way back. The sky, sun, air and the trees were all good fellows. They had speech. They had touch. They knew 'good'. They knew God.

3.

Truth just happens

7 had a flower's restlessness. The sound I needed to
hear was, 'Sir there's a call for you' but the afternoon,
out of long practice, put me into sleep heaven where I
made sleep babies. It was interrupted by a knock and *the*
announcement. Suffering from the consequences of sleep,
I stumbled down to the ground floor house and received
destiny by picking up the receiver. It was an order, given in
death's voice. 'Come to Dhakka Colony, Kingsway Camp,
right now!' Remote little Venuses stopped crumpling
under me immediately. It was a warning. 'Don't!' Some
neurological part whispered, 'What are you getting into?
Aren't you unloved enough? Put on your far vision.
Do you want to dig your own grave?' In spite of that, I
made a human choice. You don't tell water what to do
when it reaches a downward slope. I fastened myself to
the twilight and stepped out. Sublime rivers of patience,
however, became dry looking for 'Dhakka Colony in
Kingsway Cantt.' I was turning against this tale when I
decided to ask just one more fellow who might have the
knowledge of my compass and he was idling away time
against the pavement by exploring his auto's underside.
His maturity was the truth of that day. He had no issues
with anyone in this life. Everyone makes mistakes. He

7

corrected me. 'This is Cantt. Kingsway Camp is there!' His lever like arm poised in a vague direction. To add to the special effect, I turned and looked. He had a talent for beyond but espied my talent for hesitation. 'Give me a minute.' That with practiced sociability, then gently lowering the auto, he stepped on the accelerator and I entered his beautiful mind where the day swung into shadows back and forth constantly, sometimes he returned, sometimes he didn't.

When he didn't, the goal seemed out of reach and when he did, I got a wandering feel and I had to use language. How long? How far? How short? How close? He didn't speak much. He was a man born from shadows, cutting through light was only a trick. 'You will reach your destination shortly.' I had no idea that he would immediately straighten out the lies of narrow and twisted passages that made the old mosaics of the spent medieval darkness of North Delhi. 'This is it.' He stopped outside a very provincial looking gate. I got out, paid him and showed my appreciation for his effort and skills with a thin poem of thanks. The door was opened by my future MIL; a woman turned to rusty iron over the years. Her mythology was that she used to have a head that was so swollen due to its bun that I don't think it could have been held in place by anyone other than her. She never even used it to take all those instant decisions she did from time to time. The second feature was her voice, a walled city kind of voice, the death voice I had heard on the phone. It hurt to hear her. Terse with a suddenness. She ruled with it. She engaged me with it. 'Come to the other gate.' My bravado was invisible in the darkness. I reminded myself that it was the house of my hope, the house of the beautiful and proceeded through the tall grass of the courtyard to the other gate at the back and was led through the dining room into the drawing room where I sat like penniless audience until *her* name was announced. From the vast insurgency of names, Kaia was the one I fell in love with but when Kaia came and sat opposite me, she began to study the ceiling and the walls. Part of feminine courtesy, I supposed.

Anyway, it helped me to skip the symbolism of her simplicity. Truth never asserts itself. Had I rehearsed my speeches? No. The only rehearsed part of my talk has always been much movement of hands. Did I experience speech failure? No. This was not yet in my list of horrors. Was I articulate? There was no need. Did the questions and answers work in my favour? Can't tell. Kaia just didn't seem motivated to marry. Was I qualified to wear the ring? I was hardly qualified to be human. Describe the girl. Well, since I had some misconceptions about dress, she was in a red and black shalwar suit style of a time when lilies existed as far back as Solomon. Describe yourself. Since fashion needs no compassion, I would be straightforward. I learnt (later) that my appearance was the subject of much comedy between her and her sister. And why? Well, first I presented myself with, what you would call, the look of education by all the talk of my madness for books. But when it reached its limit, my hair packed into place with mustard oil, became visible, followed by my dress which comprised a pair of jeans topped by a plain t-shirt, a pair of low budget sockless shoes and my terrible laughter which happened because in Kaia's beautiful world, I forgot I was unconventionally ugly.

Now dinner was law as far as MIL was concerned. I tried saying no but she quashed it with the force of her sheer good will. 'It's only a simple meal,' she assured me. I was not in proper dinner-wear and it contrasted with MIL's proper prospective-mother-in-law-wear. She had made the occasion an absolutely casual affair with deep sunset china plates. I treated her meat curry with great respect by filling my plate and holding the morsels by their heels, drowned one after another into it. Kaia and I sat like a dinner couple. I don't know whether she and MIL were watching me but I became louder and louder with the chops while she grew quieter and quieter with a virtual form of eating I had never witnessed anywhere. I couldn't help it. With my burnt funniness on top like the crust of a fruitcake, I tried to point out, while finishing my fifth or sixth chapatti, that she had not even finished one. She raised her eyes and shot down my concern with cold and hard sarcasm, 'Are you counting mine?' It doesn't take long to finish a free dinner but I had been somewhat lingering on it, however, after that good bit of theater from Kaia, I felt no resistance but to hurry up. I skipped a few etiquettes and straightaway announced that it was ten o'clock and that I had to make a marathon journey by several buses back to Mehrauli. MIL and Kaia showed it in their nature to be polite in getting up immediately and opening the door and the gate and letting me out into that October night.

It was not just another night. It was a new night. It made the air smell of MIL's food. It made the road gleam like day. It made the city drunk on dreams. It eclipsed my sleep. It ended my marriage to Loneliness. The room was lighted up by the night, in the darkness of Mehrauli.

Past its midpoint, it deepened like a woman, taking the mercury up and distancing me from the rest of humanity. How delirious were the stars where I lay in my bed and could not sleep since the bed melted under me and so I got up and filled some of my empty writings and paintings with the greed of love and of the events that had taken place, since night never remembers what it was yesterday and with that I took it to the workaday morning. When I stepped out, night now deep in the recesses of my eyes, my landlady, Mrs. Mishra asked me her name and when I told her, she showed broad daylight in her smile and repeated the name, Kaaaaaaiiiiiiiiiiiiiiiiiiaaaaaaaaaaaaaa, making it sound like this narrative, at the end of which she said, 'That is the girl for you! You make your bed with her!' I didn't know that life is a virgin every moment. It breaks on you with orgasmic surprise. My appetite knew no joy when I was summoned again. A goodbye to Mehrauli lay in my walk as I went down the slope from her house, a most willing walk every time I was called. I travelled by telepathy, learning that I could reach Kaia either way from AIIMS and didn't mind making a whole round trip of the ring road. Mudrika was quite a symbolic discovery. I have never wished for the ordinary.

The second meeting was dominated by Kaia's elder sister. To call Rita just a woman would be an understatement. She was a world drawn to perfection. An epitome of international image, resourcefulness and fashion-first. The dresses always put her audience in a sort of tension. She intervened by arriving from England in November and turned it into a celebration month, meeting at meals as often as she summoned me. The experience of warming up to the truly Corporate Woman was a milestone achievement for me. The Priestess of Manners inhaled my carbon dioxide and called it oxygen. In other words, she called me sweet and cute. I was smitten by the haute couture of G 39, Dhakka Colony, because Kaia, my heart was on a skateboard and rolled after her, hauled her pretty ass about in denim, her top socially enhanced by a t-shirt, her hair open for action as in a thriller, her eyes, cheeks and lips made up in plus-fashion. The last thing that I had never dreamed of, was meeting his Excellency, the former viceroy of an erstwhile British colony, Sir Adam Roe, a most thorough gentleman of British finish. I felt like a native in the company of that higher edition of humanity. I honored his presence by not speaking much, in fact, I sat in woody perfection, trying to camouflage with the furniture etc. I hardly moved my mandibles when it came to dining at genteel places like The Maidens. He tried his best to include me into his knowledge of the world in those brief but long meetings, made severe with heavy smoking but I had convinced myself that truth is just ignorance and ordered the soup like them to show that one's knowledge is a lie and that I had no tricks about me except fluctuating bits of English with which they, especially the former viceroy, were trying to connect with me. They never juggled their eyes to judge me in my t-shirt and jeans and shoes without socks and hair in oil. But it all helped as I ended up generating so much of their faith in me that they convinced Kaia that I was the guy for her and I was thankful that I had a family for the Sundays if not the entire weekend.

The following weekend, I realized that all the roads to MIL's home were paved with relatives. Prudence warned me of the lots of journeys I would have to make in the years to come to be fully acquainted with all of them. Rita and the former viceroy had the option of wings. She sensed my mood, 'Stand you! In the middle! You'd better look at everyone here; you are going to be related to them very soon.' I thanked her for the opportunity. 'Welcome,' whispered the viceroy, 'Stereotypes are not allowed here.' Rita and Kaia helped me to sort out the aunts, uncles, Bhaiya, Bhabhis and cousins. I shook a mile of hands, observing and remembering each nick name and characteristic. Uncle Jean (he had offered his clandestine services to check my shadowy background), an alpha male. His wife, spicy aunt Milly. Their son Nero, handsome as one shed from a pale dream; his masculinity as thin as parchment. Aunt Privy with her stories and speeches that transcended time and space. Her husband, uncle Abe, soft as cotton. Their two sons were like two chieftains with whom I shared a tickle or two over mutual viewpoints. Giddy Bhabhi on whom makeup didn't work because she was white like light. Her husband, Raja Bhaiya, exalted by his displaced sense of humor. Aunt Holly, an AIIMS veteran, the Martha of the family. She claimed she was the only one with brains in the whole clan. Aunt Little, with her private love for Kaia, soothing like nylon night. Uncle Fizzy, a most remarkable man but greatly underrated, tough and savory as rock-salt. The only thing he had not done was accompany Ulysses on his Odyssey. The last three wore their mantle of renunciation, made from the same cloth as the one from which their virgin ancestors were made. Vigo Bhaiya, a man bathroom-thirsty for alcohol. His wife Julep, who was not even water-indulgent. Undo

Bhai and his family were absent. He was harvesting gold in some Arab country. I was humbled and never reached the point of speech.

The great culture of food at G-39 was as great as my mother's but MIL's involved a kind of food violence. She food-terrorized his Excellency, the former viceroy, Sir Adam Roe. She thought, the only way for one to be happy in this world was to fear her repeatedly large servings of pulao, meat curry, paneer gravy, kebabs and what not. The festival of happiness was organized for everyone to celebrate the annual visit of the former viceroy and his wife and the latter tried their best to mix their oil with water. Neither was I relative material. I was there for Kaia and was happy to see that her food roots were deep because, besides MIL, at every food day, like this one, everyone eulogized Rita and Kaia's dad. The fond memories this great man evoked, were partly due to his connection to food. He was known to bring all the relatives to the point of affectionate unity by his cooking. He would have passed on his food education to Kaia, but the father of this great food community left life behind as early as 1980. An occasional smile from me to her conveyed that I was quite impressed but she looked back at me like Alice forgotten in her own wonderland. In that climate of eating, drinking and merry-making, she was completely food disconnected. By the time I left, I had become a food citizen of that world and tried to escape Mrs. Mishra's notice but I might as well have been an escaping whale. She was always there in the veranda and said, 'You look like a man shaped by food today!'

4.
Wedding is not even part knowledge

*A*s winter turned more invincibly thorny, Rita and the viceroy softened towards me even more and in a meeting in the middle of the first week engaged my interest with an unsuspecting question, 'Would you like to be made captive before we take off by the end of this month?' It took me an effort to pick the right look of modesty to answer that one. 'On 18th.' That extorted a laugh or two from them. 'No! That's too early! However, whatever date you choose, it has to be a Wednesday by policy.' But my life needed plumbing as early as possible. 'Then 25th!' And that date definitely got their excitement and their agreement. I wet my lips. 'So, now what?' MIL, who did not inspire glamour, being so straightforward, said, 'So now, you inform your mother.' I was in a creative age, the oil in my head made it work, hence, instead of phoning her, I sent a phonogram to my mother: GIRL WANTS WEDDING ON TWENTYFIFTH. After that I partied blindly. The breakthrough was Kaia. I felt this incredible rush to board the buses, roaming the hitherto homeless city. Its closed ways opened and handed the world to me the whole day and even far into the night, beginning to grow in the direction of galaxies. Life became space. Stars came close. The three hands of the wristwatch drew handfuls of eternity from time's reservoirs. Very soon I was acting like a dreamer. I had known fragrant women before. I was familiar with the strategies of the beautiful. But Kaia? She extorted everything from me. I lived on her looks when she sat next to me, paring my nails. Thin aesthetics covered her like a skin. She was the possessor of an affluent world of unseen flowers and unheard streams. A summer's new sizzling inviting worlds. A winter's unfelt warmth. A rainforest's untouched, unsounded bells. Unthinkable fields full of unharvested grain.

She was becoming my fiction that had to be made real with the teen act of phoning in the mornings from General Raj's reception. Her voice? Imagine dawn, with sleep included, as wine. I was drunk the whole day. The landline became my love platform from where I murmured to her, in a new voice every day, my poetry and what it made of her beauty, hoping and praying that her beauty would make something of my poetry. I martyred my talent resonating each verse with intimate elegance but its borders were torched with passionate eroticism. Hence, when I met her, I looked deep into her eyes to try to fathom the moving emotion I had felt when writing them but all I found was a suffering essay on how she bravely faced them all alone. People looked at me and wondered why I had become so sweet. I told them I was having only honey. I kept the moon for another day. Kaia performed a love trick on me by laughing once or twice at my unmarried humor but the very sight of her free laughter was quite a physical, intellectual and spiritual fortune. It lit the moonlight when I stepped out of the house. It forced the sunrise over my room in Mehrauli. I joined my love to it and that involved my heart and mind twenty-four hours. Love is second faith. It made school easier. My disgust for the principal's PA, Mrs. Moy, whom I considered a witch, and my fear of the principal were transformed into admiration. I was drunk on this new world. I wanted time to move forward faster but it seemed to entertain itself by slowing down or sometimes even backing up. Gravity seemed to disappear between me and the earth. I had no weight. The whole world was on a downward slope.

The hues of love on me, made me be counted among the living. My eye world contracted to seeing only her and in it she became large as light. If you can have food by aroma, then I was having her. Only by sight, smell and sometimes an accidental or deliberate touch. In the meeting on 14th, the girls, so far busy in all the fun, suddenly changed the love-chew talk into serious discussion. '25th is not far! Your mother has not replied!!' When I didn't answer, those three women, MIL, Rita and Kaia, so effective when put together, told me to stay the night, which I did, and to travel the next morning. 'You have to go and ask for your mother's permission. We don't want to be accused of coercion.' That meant road fatigue because I was not a man of travel. They checked the edges of my travel preparations in the morning and held a doodle meeting over me with MIL fussing with journey food and Kaia fetching her rice jacket for me and Rita and the viceroy ensuring that it fitted me. In the world's backyard, I remembered, there was a thing called home with a mother always on the horizon. To perfect the meeting, I took a picture of Kaia. A free poet's soul travels ahead in time. I perceived my mother ascending and descending the length, breadth and width of the house with her work face, a picture of classical transparency, permissible love, controlled charm, self-discipline and the evidence of champions in everything she did. So, when the day changed its course, I reached Hategarh and the bus entered the thin country of Barhpur and old time came out and met me as I stepped into the house opposite the Pipal Tree.

Time's idea of mothers is that they don't grow old but when they do, they become an era. The evening did look older around her even though I was not meeting her in years but as the wine of the last meeting with a loved one goes down quick, so it was that it seemed that predictability did not fail me too. I was in two states when she asked me, 'What brings you here all of a sudden?' Forthwith I cut the conventions of conversation and produced my love shield, Kaia's picture, and conscious of my elder brother (a captive of my written words, the mythological one, perceiving everything from his mythological edges) and sister watching and listening, said, 'It is not my turn to get married but there is this girl. She wants to. Didn't you get my phonogram?' She looked at the picture, one couldn't say whether it was in positive or negative speculation and said, 'I did but it said GIRL WANTS BEDDING BY TWENTYFIFTH!' Those humans at post offices and other government departments are such delightful people. I withdrew the photograph of the girl who wanted her bedding by twenty fifth. In green grass's experience, the sky is always above it and so was she. A non-citizen of this world, she watched my new happiness with her eyes of an old empress. 'One week is short notice but I will see to all the arrangements for your wedding.' And so, going by the culture of kisses, I planted one on her cheek and left with seducing intensity to seriously invest in life in the coming days. It was a one-day wind trip between those two places.

The DTC bus, a sunset sister of the sunrise one, now stood on the edge of the wind and the latter is totally a woman too, I am sure. She stripped the sunset in no time and out came night, pushed in virgin verses before my eyes. Each second was a mock picture of another from which the coming days would take birth. When the all-night poetry was finished, love's thrill began to sing its tale in my looks. There was a verse week of happiness for me to get my date-face right before I could push the ring up Kaia's finger. But first came November 18. No, it is not a vacuum. The clearest detail I remember of my birth is that when my father had gone away to do M.Sc., my mother had me; her fourth kid. She was the only one who made us all feel the magic of growing that culminated on our birthdays with lavish meals and new clothes. Except her, I have never been invited to my birthday party if ever there had been one thrown by anyone else but when Kaia and Rita, both headful beauties, came on the scene, they shampoo-mocked me. 'Give your hair an oil break and get a shampooed look,' they said as they presented me Head and Shoulders. But my real gift was a wife one week from thence. Now my hair had had a partnership with oil since childhood and if I did not put it, the wind fueled them. So, it was not completely off and also not so much that when I met them next, they did not feel that I could cause an oil drizzle. Then 20th brought me my sister, brother and my mother - with the edges of years like that of a time traveler, on her face of many commitments.

And when the relatives came, I ceased to feel like a boy anymore because then the moments of myth took over.

Yes, those are there even in an Indian Christian wedding. The whole family gets an opportunity to act as a creative group to wrap up the bride or the bridegroom's bodies except the love parts in oils and condiments. For me it was a visual experience to see my coalman's face improve slightly so that I could fit into the thresholds of the white veiled bride. On 22nd there was a desperate hunt for a house because Vigo, Kaia's brother with the bottle connection, asked me where I would take my bride after the wedding and so I flung aside the beautiful time one day and searched the cityscape for a house, finally sniffing at one in Gautam Nagar but the women united against it. At the end it was Vigo who managed the whole action of finding me one in Nirarkari Colony, a whistle away from Dhakka Colony. A predictable house with a grilled hole in the roof that connected the imagination of the voyeuristic landlord on his ground floor with his tenants' lives on the first. He possibly hoped to catch neon sounds of the night like repeating laughter from amorous love-making or during the day, the under-display of an exotic raging-red negligee.

A wedding is a story thing. Past midnight, dying the night in its colours is the dream dust that begins to fall and the day receives its festive look. All the years of celebration in a century become concentrated in one day. May stones blame the church for giving so much importance to a mere man and woman! We were in separate trances on the wedding day. She was locked in a tight town of anxiety and I was chasing continents of euphoria and building cities of inspiration. The details of the wedding day are that I have never been more desperate for church (I guess, it is easier to be the bridegroom). That the women were perfumed and powdered blind. The bride looked another version of the divine, unleashing sparkle into an already bright day. For MIL, on any other day, house was habit but that day she was on tight lips, fitting her routine motherly and mother-in-law duties into the chaos. Caught in it were Rita and the former viceroy, eliminating all worries with their traveler's cheques. The wedding moved like words in this book. I sensed the woman coming my way up the aisle, a whole big city of relatives pushing her train. Her gait was a half walk of singing art and the other half, literary magic, skin merging into her clothes, a twinkly fit from stars that ended on butterflies and candle dust covered hearts with wings. Her silk and her perfume swelled around her, invading and transforming vintage vales of the same in the pews. Blooms in the bouquets bowed to the goddess, bringing love to the love doomed. I'm sure there's something about a bride in white that you can say is fine-tuned to the point of being morally pretty. It is the right kind of atonement for worldly men like me and the longest songs are played at funerals and weddings but this one was a meeting of life around a ring. The book-eyed priest knew his beard and went through the costumed drama.

Oh! Breath-beautiful she was when we came as close as a kiss, that is the very wine of marriage which I would taste in a few minutes. My acting friends from the church were there. Our families sat in the pews on sepia display. On the spur of the Bride's light stood the

Bridesmaid. Sumer, my Best Man remained my faithful soldier throughout the whole wedding poetry. We collected around the ring and the priest ran us through his old book of *I dos*. We were herded into the vestry and further married into a book of signatures. For the first time, I had the bride in my possession as I lifted her veil and kissed her. The wedded walk to the door began with confetti exploding around us like little festivals which culminated in a siege at the door. Benign crowds of relatives and friends took turns to be caught up in Kaia's essence, leaving no scope for a hugging or kissing gap for anyone else. Somebody's face was always getting in front of mine. Finally, I made necessary escape with the shining love icon to a studio for a photograph on more elevated paper. A first-time bride and a first-time bridegroom we were but the difference was: I was only meeting the change whereas she was already the future. Makeup is the skin that marriage wears with a white gown in the church and a rich red gold sari at dinner. Kaia was quiet as champagne but I had found a new dream. With my bride on my side, our smiles shared and our arms linked, I was ready, though she took the front of most conversation. An endless line of well-wishers, relatives, friends, acquaintances and even strangers pimped us for a kiss and a handshake. Between cake-cutting and the dinner, the evening's essence was captured by a live English band in whose music dancing young pairs eroded their breaths. The whole programme was documented but when the video man's blinding light passed over me, Kaia's cousin, the future Mr. Wendy Peters, detected a visual and smiling soundlessly he began to make his way towards me through the crowd.

The food festival had turned effete. The former viceroy joined the guitarists. Yogesh sang his swallow song. Someone served me a unique wedding experience on a plate in the shape of only a cauliflower. The viceroy descended and there was a shortage of stars in the heavens when he and Rita performed a dance of extreme fidelity. I got encouraged and tried my mucus at a song and was about to evolve into a higher form when the cousin reached me and whispered in my ear. I heard him like the blind and then looked down like the deaf. A door was open in my dinner suit's trouser, very much like my mouth. It was such a pre-Christian sight! My cities of inspiration abandoned me and the continents shrank. I am still persecuted by the memory. And that is why, I say, that the unknown exists as a firstborn. The surprises keep coming. When the features of the wedding began to weaken, I went down for a cup of coffee where the light did not follow me and the fellow refused me at my own banquet. The *vidai* was a hybrid of wedding tears. Meadows were lost when Kaia shed a few and at that Sully, my brother-in-law, also wiped his eyes. My Dididi, offered some warmth to Kaia's cold hands. Uncle Doug, who was always at the back like a great myth master, gave us his car to take us to his house.

As we left, the town dust began to reclaim the town.

At the house on Baba Kharak Singh Marg, the insanity of the coming moments slowly descended on us and a linguistic lethargy on those whose goal was to engage us in an endless conversation. Finally, night locked itself around both of us in a bedroom and there was a feeling that I not only had the complete possession of the bride but she was finally within reach of my hugs and some tactile fun at least if not the whole nine yards in one night. The former viceroy had ensured that I attended preschool where he taught me that I would need a month of women for an hour of that experience with a new bride. Kaia didn't allow me to drop my clothes or hers but gradually we worked on our curiosities and our bodies came close and when our clothes deteriorated completely into wrinkles, her eye mounds began to roll on a dream track along which moonbeams sat. Night passed and the sun flowered on gliding smiles of two mortal virgins. But that evening, love was the road my mother took back home and I could not even see her off. She waited and waited for me at the bus station until Aru said, 'Ma, he's not coming.' That was one sunset that would always be missing from my life. A day breaking loneliness followed that emptiness. That vacuum. When I got back to G 39 from Mehrauli with all my stuff, I faced a moment of ice in her face and water in her eyes when Kaia opened the door. Her sister had joked that I wasn't coming back ever. In the living room, hard men and harder women were giving in to the pleasures of the bottle. I was the only mortal in their presence, not able to kill a single drink. Instead, I tried to pass a smile around, until Vigo, with whisky in his voice and feet on the table, challenged me saying, 'Abe yaar, aurte bhi pi rahi hain…!' I survived that by pouring the contents into his shoes.

Next day, we moved into the honeymoon house, filled to the brim with the wedding world's wealth.

5.

Solar marriage lunar bed

A wedding's requirement is bedroom first. It was all the consequences of eyes. I saw her as the female at my threshold. That was the visible woman. The invisible one was the change-maker. This was a sudden area of life's experiences. It split me further. Now a life dreamer emerged onto the scene, lost in a woman's inexperienced body magic. Her young fingers, however, were not without experience. She made one vegetable and a few chapattis and then got into her bridal fashion, smiled at me from behind her foundation and left for her office. With wordless eyes I studied her, processing her as a possible book in my head; she was its chief character; its text was assured because she was it, a book that was long in its tale; I could not see if it had an ending. Then the weekend came and in the ambiguity of its hours, I explained to her the reason for my pleasure. I said, 'Your sabzee is amazing and I cannot ask for more delight but I have grown up in a house of regular meals. Momentous lunches were our identity.' The household girl had not yet emerged from its cocoon. Work attack was as yet taking shape. And there I was emotionally overwhelming her. She had surrounded herself with clothes from her several suitcases on the floor and asked me, 'What is a momentous lunch?' I laughed and said, 'Oh that! It's just a traditional one with dal, rice, sabzee, roti and salad.' It was then that she looked at me properly for the first time and love became an error. Beauty died. Romance lost its qualities. I watched her face closely and a very gradual change came over her features. The eyes began to ooze and in the midst of her countenance, dissipating into something which even an animation artist like me could not have imagined, she cried, 'I cannot do it! I cannot make traditional, momentous lunches!!'

Oh! What a shot of stupidity I had given myself! But then, if a woman's eyes are a problem, a man's careful words can be the solution. With incredible kindness, I have not been able to replicate ever since, I too cried out, 'Oh my perfidious past! Oh! My years of darkness!! Why did I mention that? Don't worry,' I promised in the same breath, 'If you are beautiful then I am talented, I will make the traditional lunch, you won't have to worry about a thing! Now stop crying.' She did that immediately. And since then, I have kept my promise, never ever missing my conservative lunch for which she also developed a conceptual approach first and then fell in love with it on weekends. We began to meet in the kitchen too. Then I left, in the heat of the winter morning with visions of her in drought garments. The city fell into place around me, organizing itself into roads and buildings and traffic and I knew she was my tale who had met her guy, the author. I was a love priest. She was my goddess. Love is in the face but a woman's soul is in her clothes too and so when I got back, I moved from utopia to utopia. I felt her in the unlimited lunch and then in the divine luxury of the afternoon bed, absorbed completely into the flavors of her clothes, which were cast carelessly across the bed.

I listened for her footsteps with ears of love or stood in the balcony with eyes of love, watching a love sunset behind her as she walked from the turning. For a few moments, she remained a company girl, sharing with me the day's events over dinner. Then we changed to love's Latin and Greek and then at the end, we placed ourselves under the night and I became her first Adam and she my first Eve and I discovered that infinity is not time.

Night was a girl. Young and pretty. She deepened around twelve. By dawn, a woman, growing hot by midday. And before she was ready again for a repeat, she gave birth to her offspring. Dusk. The moonlight hung dim like an old light outside, against which each moment was built in whispers of melody. Sometimes religious. A walk with angels. Sometimes secular. A resonating weekend. Whatever it was, we made colours of the rainbow within the four walls of the house and where also the stars appeared at night. In short, we didn't go out anywhere . She knew she was love-beheld, dancing her weight in light rhythm, a siren with the organic ease of humans. A dancing sunset rose and dipped, rose and dipped until the fun reached its climax. Then the dance winds subsided and against a slow and gentle background of late night, All India Radio began to play its lullabies of sorrow. It rolled us back into those times when music was still respectable and the girl in the song and the dance allowed herself to be carried away by the town's many sad rivers to join hundreds of thousands of others who had no other wish but to drown and die in the sad songs of Mukesh, Kishor, Rafi and a few others.

Pathos as quickly dead and infinity and time resumed, stifling the muse....

6.

A little pace in a closet marriage

*W*omen are built like bees. They come to the earth with the serious aim to only work. The mother-in-law of many landscapes was no exception. In the third week, MIL made her appearance, to put a little pace into the story here, and presented Kaia with what seemed to be a rude version of a wooden bat. I didn't think it was for me even though I have always been in good need of a drubbing every now and then. Anyway, the pitch was set and it was too late to reverse things. Besides, my marriage was nothing short of a small hard miracle so I decided to bawl or bat or if asked even field. I took it as a positive development, something that would give me a chance to prove to myself that I was game for anything. If it was work, then I was already trying to reach a fuller work understanding, enabling rice and dal to boil. If it was anything else, I dealt with it by overcoming it with creative intensity. Of course, I was no match to Kaia. Her battledress was her lingerie; when she appeared in it, I lay prostrate. Without it, however, she shone like an albino in the darkness. Or in daylight, like full cups of vanilla. The fragile, fragrant Venus (she transformed at will) maintained her vanilla by exploring the use of anti-uv creams on her small hands and feet at night before going to bed. The wooden tool, however, made its presence felt one day when the v hours of the morning got into dire straits. I woke up to the sound of ancient rhythms, quite outside my body, nay, outside our bedroom. My Vanilla was not in bed. It couldn't have been convention or I would have known. Anyway, it drew me out of bed. I was some Keats watching with half eyes, my thing of beauty pounding clothes with violent antagonism in the bathroom with that prosaic implement. Now, men are controlled by their pastime and women by their energy and in every culture, I believe, they use their energy to communicate with their men but ever since the arrival of language in the world, there should be no need, I felt, for a mute force of that magnitude to be used to communicate with anyone but I got the message and so also the landlord since the whole building was freed from the deep hold of slumber. No wonder, he came up with the sun but she stood voicelessly in her raging-red negligee when he requested her not to wash clothes at five. Next morning, the house detonated with her clothes rioting two hours earlier than the previous morning. The landlord knew that Kaia's baton was up. In fact, he lighted an incense stick when the inauspicious hour began.

7.

An organizational dictator

I accepted female domination by tunic and wore the mantel of my marriage but not like a slave's since I was a radical and was never at apology. She was never at apology too but she was not a revolutionary. She, however, had revolutionary support. From MIL, her senior version. The latter was an organizational dictator and, hence, a global one too. She became, by mid-December, our weekend officer. Faithfully and punctually, she reported for duty, that being, to seriously invest in our relationship as if she was on our marriage staff. So now, we were the world's responsibility and I had no idea, that how, when, where and by whom, the decision was taken to move us from there to a property, MIL owned. Well, atoms and molecules dwelt in me too. I opposed the move but to no avail. Need of a home of our own was not an easy dream. The monthly rent of rupees two thousand gave Kaia a stronger argument. It was less of a home, she felt, where, at the start of each month, I had to give away a good part of my salary to the landlord and money in those days was of the tight kind.

I lost that round. It led to change of scenery.

8.
New and incomplete

*M*IL, leader of our landscape, led us there one day. From the twisted streets of Delhi, we entered the straight, visionless roads of Rohini, opening into an isolation world. The place was a vacuum. A private tradition-less planet. Everything was new and incomplete. In fact, the new and the incomplete did not leave us for quite some time. We were in a raw building with holes for doors in all other houses except ours. On the day we were to move in, there was a possession fight, that is, the guard closed the gates and I couldn't get the luggage truck in. I came up to B-30. MIL and Kaia were working, the former a champion of cleaning, dusting and washing and the latter an artist of creation. I told them that I was up against the impossible. Tradition for MIL was an instant. So in an instant, with death's blazes in her eyes, face and on her tongue, she rolled up her sleeves and punched a hole in what I had thought was 'the impossible'. The guard had never seen a metal so hard, an energy so dominant, an act so violent, a will so strong; he heaved himself out of her way just in time and the huge and heavy gates yielded like a triviality to the naked force of her hurricane hands. Frogs of joy broke from hibernation and leaped out of me as I preceded the truck into the society. She could have moved a mountain and not by faith too. After imparting her mother's training to Kaia, she left and I felt more settled. Next day, I got up early and followed the day around. A lot is founded in those hours for early is a song. Its details are in the passion each leaf has for life as it dances; it is the total experience of spiritual love. Why, love is learnt even when fingertips touch. Hence, each creature becomes the next artist of love. Each star takes birth in love's moments and even death becomes the art of nothingness. And yet we have to rework life every day.

In the world of humans, there wouldn't be any song, dance and love without having to work for it. Hence, I started the day with a cuppa chai for both of us. Laughter flows in a good cup of tea. An honest beginning of the day is made with it, at least. I tapped the spirituality of love, collected in each sip, a practice I have not given up ever since it began when I began to access God's melodies in the morning; for God is a singer too and God is a lover too and God has the best moves. From the nursery of dreams, she too woke up and catching her clothes on, came and joined me in my school where I was learning to feel that we were together and that we had to impact the lives that proceeded from us to experience the incredible thing called family and that can only come from the Father of happiness who put it there deep in Adam and Eve. I was a woman's responsibility but by late evening, I had one too. To pick her up after she arrived by bus from her office. It was still winter and it grew dark very quickly. I have always been hyperconscious of the night but there it was unblessed and even the sun rose over it with some fear. It so grew like a goliath and I, a little David, toured it and ran about in it for five days of the week. The road to rudimentary right angles seemed to hold the very ends of the earth. I learnt that the planet was a lonely place and not very explorable on the back of a rickshawman but we went around, until we had made enough night spaghetti, finally getting to that part where Kaia was standing and waiting for me. She and I were two nervous beings who left the ends of the night, somehow sharper and whiter like pointed teeth. There was no question whether the night would come or not the next day. It was night anytime she went out but night was my responsibility. I hung a naked bulb at the end of a long wire from the second-floor balcony though night had no respect for any form of lighting (night is judged and punished for this during a wild and wet storm). Marriage was our new identity and we resumed our time, chasing the goals of love and setting the scene to celebrate and enjoy its traditions. Dinner for many years became law and she also made her talking-time with stories about her office. Darkness, after midnight in that house, was a long zombie phenomenon, invented by rats and not without their own music, the type psychological vermin recognize. Like a strange slowness that grows out of the conscience, they made their entry from mysterious spaces, a faint cast with spent features, onto the theater of the strange.

They were an anonymous people but not without voices, flawed faces, arched backs and attitude-hairstyles. They circled wagons of explorers and pioneers. They imperiled the very existence of civilization. When earth was a baby and matter sucked milk in some exotic age of not yet new beginnings, why, they were there, unaesthetic giants that darkened God's cities with perennial suspicion. When humanity walked for miles and miles when the grass was long and when their feet wore it out, why, they were there, stealing since then love, faith, trust, laughter, food, clothing, games, thoughts, freedom, films, applause, faces, feet, toes, beauty, boxes, walls, holes, roles, accents, potential, bodies, writings, future, scripts, brother, subconscious, sheep, universe, luck, objectivity, science, questions, cycles, years, imagination, votes, comics, shoes, sunshine, pathways, bones, colors, evidence, coffee, universities, houses, doors, change, noses, principles, time, pizzas, bathtubs, understanding, boys, metaphysics, ability, nature, collections, ground, space, photos, technology, matter, roads, simplicity, lyrics, education, calm, stories, youth, benches, sister, anything, footsteps, opportunities, heart, soundtracks, nuclear bombs, toys, thrill, work, reviews, something, breath, America, sweets, heroes, surprise, depth, both my parents. Even Moses. And they also made my fiction ugly but funny because they approached Kaia to nibble her toes, however, they were afraid to do so because she worked for a snake corporation.

The only way to escape from the misery they brought was to exterminate them from our home and so every night, I waited for them from the peak of priority. I became job proud in this. They had the night; I had the determination. I played with sleep until a clumsy hole in the night, where the exhaust fan was fitted in the kitchen, parted and a sound, I recognized, untangled itself from the silence. Those were the convulsive cues for me to change from a sublime and sober lover of truth, light and beauty into a rat's worst nightmare, namely, its most painfully and dreadfully prolonged torture before death. You have to find the devotion, I say. It was only human to battle the growing menace. I was being true to myself. This was my main business on earth: to kill. For this I needed the night. The night needed me. I could kill anytime and that was night. I hid many tight secrets of things committed deep in nights like those including the killings. In fact, I killed so much and so unpityingly that even night had to take an off to dissociate itself from me. That made me realise that people like me shouldn't have time and shouldn't have a home and don't deserve the good things of life like a family. I needed redemption. Well, if they knew how to surrender, those rats, they would have surrendered. Killing them was therapeutic for me. I was a practiced killer. I was self-taught. In my unacceptable night, first I simply caught them with a cloth, smothered them and then tossed them to the floor with all my might but when the biggest and the ugliest ones began to come in, I institutionalized death with something more sinister.

Leader of life is certainly a better individual. That is my wife but she hated rats. In fact, they frightened her. The universe is a virtual place, because we read about it. Likewise conscience. It is virtual. I don't know how it works. To attempt to put the fear of God into someone or something is a matter of conscience. Conscience has a beginning in fear of who or what we are and who or what we might become and this is also tested against who or what another is. The truth is that I was a monster but I also had specters from Constantia that haunted me. The abstract was at work. The unreasonable heart wanted to go in a different direction. It has fascination for new beginnings. It was searching the landscape for meaning. That decided the mood. And mood is never true. I was afraid to be identified. That made me the odd man out.

I was against collective culture. I was tired of smiling at relatives. It was a cancer. I was blinded. I wreaked my vengeance on the rats. They felt my wrath. After trapping them, I electrocuted them to hurt their hearts and to listen to their screams and to watch them shake and as the levers of liberty and life were about to shift, I knew that pain, fear and death are real. At the end, I burnt them. After a daily rat never returned home, their community, in the labyrinths of sector 13, Rohini, understood that they had to beware house number B-30 of Delhi Citizen Society.

Living is everything and the young want to live by everything but for that you need free time and Kaia wanted some too. She insisted on getting her a servant. The Pahari women were like pictures with a clue hidden in their looks. We met one after another but Kaia rejected them all. Later she rang up her mother and sister and described them, 'I can't keep any of them, they are all so beautiful!' The search finally led us to the house on top of us. The door was somehow hinged into place and was unhinged by one, a man that is, whose kind of ugliness is forbidden in our universe. You can get proud of such a thing and, I suspect, he was proud. Behind him, in the woods, yes, that is true, woods in the house, around a little oil lamp, was his family crouching on the floor. Was it nature in pictures behind them? I am not sure because shaking on a point was a star far above the faint lamp light's shadows. He couldn't afford such large pictures, now could he? Could we? It was a freak world and Kaia was freaking out. Unlike me, she had never encountered a strangely alive fantastic world. They seemed to know what we wanted. 'Kamwali chahiye hai aapko?' the man asked calmly.

The living are loud. 'We don't even hear their footsteps over us, do we?' I asked Kaia when the door had been hinged into place. She did not answer my question but said this, 'For a moment I thought as I stood in that house that time did not matter.' And that made me think. I am not exaggerating, though you might think that I am, but it is true that the weirdest and the strangest alien worlds are right here on the earth with us, amongst us. Her birthday was around the corner and I learnt that it is an event that is not to be treated trivially. I neither gave her a rose nor a card but I was successful in hiding in a closet. She was my soul and found me out and said, 'It was a lovely gesture. Let's go out.' Easy for her to say such things. I could not imagine eating out, what if someone saw me doing that, stuffing food into my mouth and chewing and swallowing and holding food in my hands and using my fingers and licking and smacking and cleaning the sides of the teeth with the tongue and dropping food and smearing my mouth with something and speaking with my mouth full and not passing the food and not indulging in polite conversation between small bites and looking here and there to see if others were also looking here and there, to spot and judge clumsy eaters like me and she said, 'Nonsense! Now come along.' Well, she could eat anything, anywhere from gol gappas on a street to pizzas at Nirula's. I kind of felt a nervous happiness with her, learning new lessons all the time.

9.

Chiffon dances

*D*id it look like a relationship? I don't know. A vegetable woman said once to us, 'Aapki behen ko hisaab nahi aata hai!' as Kaia took time to do the calculations. Well, while I was trying hard to understand how the bed worked best, she was busy trying to add better experience to her newly acquired home. While I was into the love-thing, she watched me with her whale's eye. If I was all fiction, she was all nonfiction. While I fed my false life, she was doing the woman's walk, shopping and buying things to fill the house with substantial color. With infinite thrift, she dressed and defined the house in feminine ways, achieving a multiple whole of domestication until the place knew itself as home and it became a happening place for the days and evenings jammed with glossy lights. The new curtains did a chiffon dance with her because I couldn't. She tried but couldn't build a dance partner in me. No, not me. In that, I was separated from her. A dance gets me into knots or I get a dance into knots or a knot gets into the dance and so on and so forth. I had song and music. The new bedsheets blossomed with true flowers on every side which garlanded us at night and I flew from school and sought home for the world and we had long moments of home days on all the holidays and it was in that pure woman's light and delight that the love mill felt the pressure of our first child.

It was brought about by the onset of spring in which love came from two bits of clothing. One, of course, was the raging red negligee. Why, the world looked exquisite only in the flames Kaia ignited. Why, we laid up the suns, one on top of another, a pile so high that it caused an avalanche of summer days in which the days were long and wide. Why, there I dreamt the one whose name I called out also in a dream. The second bit of clothing was the Bermuda. It was a clothing that might not have helped me to make a transcendental self-discovery but it was a clothing which was symbolic of how 'far' rises to meet what is 'close' because nobody knew where it came from; a clothing whose contradictions did grip my imagination; a clothing that knew the thrift law because it was cheap; a clothing that was quite without tradition because nobody knew where it vanished after a few years. Whatever the conjectures, I sought a minute in moral memory to try to discover humanity's connection with a thing like that! I cannot imagine the viceroy enjoying the luxuries of the English Spring air, in a Bermuda. It would be a very unfortunate image if the paparazzi got hold of it! We must stick to identity and it is all right for us to invest in such clothing but I have no idea why people brought the Bermuda by tons to be sent as gifts with MIL, of all the people, in her unbelievable polka dotted sari, to his excellency, the former viceroy.

10.
A wedding of wild flowers

Summer was a bunch of wild flowers, a premised setting for young laughter, in MIL's courtyards where you relaxed your lunch and passed the world by in a word known as afternoon. Lilies still existed there and were treated as high fashion because only them we wore sometimes. You might think of it as an absence of time. It is life's first rule of happiness. The mother-cause for all this happiness was that the mother-in-law had gone away to England, with tons of Bermudas, to visit Rita and the viceroy. It was sweet March music to my ears when I heard it. But happiness is not without hurt. It preceded and then followed it. A conventional meeting of different hands helped pack up MIL's bags and we were early risers at the airport, love being NCRegional, and the pressure party gave MIL, in her unbelievable polka dotted sari hung over high heels, her media moments. Kaia strode around. At pre-dawn, she was like sunshine with a makeup, feeling long-stressed to walk, a champion of ace energy, but she was frail and that place consumed her and that walk triggered a blitz attack. I felt the fall myself with that feeling of summer that makes life a violent phenomenon. As the day was about to break, chances of a beautiful sunshine were ruined with the torture of bleeding. The day was already down before the sun even rose a peep. She was the suffering heroine and we rushed her to Dr. Veena, the gynecologist, near MIL's house. The diagnosis: threatened abortion. She had conceived and had passed through the woods of fear on paths of courage and the unborn one changed back to life because s/he was a seed that God knew but Kaia had to take care; not climb stairs which meant B-30 was out of the question, take bedrest for about two months which meant staying at G-39. A hidden population of worries awed me. This was a crisis but Good is above and God is with us. Her aunts arrived to look after her.

Kaia's aunts fixed themselves around her like a couple of sad past centuries with a perspective on how to control, plan and programme young, married and independent lives. It was only a meeting of the maidens since Aunt Holly, the lady with the little gait but with her 'Power Is Mine' looks, accompanied by misty faced aunt Little. They had not brought along with them their brother, the sad silhouetted bachelor uncle Fizzy. The third person to violate the rights of the ring, however, was aunt Sally, who looked, dressed and spoke like suburban flatulence. She often arrived from the neighborhood to complete the union of the three sisters. I didn't need mental ingenuity to deal with these invaders of marital pleasures but they made it amply manifest that they had privileges. G-39 was family area. Niece love was their life at the moment. I became life's extra and was so far removed that I began to have vague recollections of a wife. What did I exist for? After my thin slice of school, I wanted a big bite of the marriage, suffering, pain, stress, tears, all included. Kaia had changed hands. I watched Aunt Holly design the food in Kaia's plate with ritual incredibility at lunch and dinner. At breakfast she got fragmented parathas. It was only a banquet for a tiny doll that she took Kaia to be. I could not avoid being agitated. With self-prescribed feelings, emotions and thoughts of protest, as cure, I tried to make a beginning with words but since my eyes were not me, that is, I looked shy by nature and am totally not, my distress and dissent were not even recognized.

My second most venerable response was to set the ice between them and me but that too didn't work. There was no question of trying politeness and gentle manners, those being the concerns of diplomats, anymore. With an undocumentable look, therefore, I turned off their happy evening, one evening and put the sparks into the whole effort. You have to work them in the correct voice key first, by changing the veins in the neck from subtle to noticeably swollen, followed by the ones in the forehead. Next comes color or complexion, which is a very important ingredient in an Indian marriage. It must get darker and darker as the voice key grows deeper and deeper. When I had the right voice key, I pulled the darkest color possible over my face and said to them that I alone was Kaia's knight in shining armor. I was from a fighting world and my blood must have turned into gasoline because Aru, my sister, who was also visiting me, lighted a match at the right moment and out came fire from my mouth and smoke from my nostrils and even ears. If you shut out my height, then, I was a monster with hate specials brewing in my eye and mouth refineries. The burnt air couldn't be replaced afterwards, so strong was the acrid environment. That day, Kaia must have felt defeated in her relationship with me but that day I put the era forward on my marriage. The obligations of the relationship demanded that I showed them respect but I was no hot-pooled pet and crossed the limits by banging the door in their faces as well. The shock of all the violence was so literal that aunt Sally didn't even wait for the radical realization to hit her that she might be hit with more than a radical realization and escaped immediately as her house was the closest.

Little and Holly aunties also recognized the deadline for reverse withdrawal on mutual counsel, fear and possibly further humiliation. 'We have to leave while our honor is still intact.' They declared to Kaia, all jittery from the experience. I was aware that I had made my marriage smaller with that most highly embarrassing behavior but then what prevents a shark from opening its jaws and biting its prey? Kaia was a very positive partner, however. She forgot and forgave by June what had happened in May but before that she hoped that I too would feel some mature shame. There was no expiation from my side, however. 'Theater is not prohibited, is it?' I asked her, trying to kill my grimacing teeth with a sweet smile. 'You will invest the impossible into this marriage if this goes on.' I don't know why she had this fear that no relative from then on would host us or be hosted by us. 'You need to wear my brains and see things as I see them as your husband. I will not allow anyone to curb and control what my responsibilities towards you are!' I knew this argument would go into the unchecked poetry of invective soon enough if I didn't shut up and so I let her have the last word. 'Home,' she said, 'is the source of everything and for me it doesn't only include the two of us.' And that was the last word. I consented with the truth. Introspection intersects me at times now and I know that G-39 itself battled me the following month for hurting the sentiments of the sorority. Summer by this time had reached its mid-May theme, setting the tone for a month and a half long vacation. Refreshed by the risk of losing some relatives, if not all, I settled in the relieved ambience of summer holidays.

11.

Summer plays the female

Summer played the female. A fantastic woman summer is. She just picked me as her man and I just mastered her as my woman. Hometown bugs would have bitten me badly but for those festivities of summerful joys. A cool day of hot pleasures nurtured mankind. Kaia and I made the wilderness of G-39 our Eden from where we would surely be expelled, come July. Recklessness was meeting my needs but woman is the epitome of sustainable behavior. Kaia made food my education, involving me in sessions of making vegetarian and non-vegetarian meals with precision and with her urban ease encouraged me to show my high creativity by mowing the lawn grass and by bringing the flower beds into some shape and in the unsustainable noon of mid-summer June, going and fetching whatever she craved. Her hunger had a new edge by sunset. And then the night opened its wants and I did a tour of the kitchen and discovered that we were living in a house of myths. An old house of ambiguous legends with different beginnings and endings for each of its previous, current and future occupants; it changed the very concept of time. It made our love mythology-induced. In its vast holdings of the night quiet, I located generations of darkness, time's collections, right from Adam's knowledge who must have first imagined fear as a middle of the night experience. Its pervasive vocabulary, shaped out of the old acts of the fans, the lights, the switches, the fridge, the mixie and the transformer, to name a few, began to engage me during the day too; it was not only the night that was against us.

Mortal is the makeup of the immortal. Material is worn by immaterial. There's no possession. No conjuration. Insanity is a crowding of the immortal and the immaterial at the gates of the mortal and the material worlds. The night makes its statement then. Unbelievable dogs join the other omens of the disquiet, expressing in hundreds of syllables how afterlife is managed. Finding the end of such a night is very difficult. One of the known measures is putting on all the lights but when the current broke its back on a storm, as often as it could, the house exhaled air from mysterious pockets of fear. Another known measure is religion. It is the only cultural protection against primordial shapes that give us nervous minds across landscapes of fear. Occasional punishment is acceptable but an ongoing onslaught becomes the regret of history and literature. With a used cry of ritual receptive purity, I, a man of transgressions, took refuge in the sacrament of reciting the Lord's Prayer. With this invocation, except to find imperial, spiritual sustenance, I did not hope to offset anything else. I was capable of exercising acts of the body but not acts of faith. My belief rose to the occasion but my word didn't have the requisite authority. Incident after incident embarked upon the darkening days. Kaia's efforts in this period were to do well by food, a surreal citizen of a different existence, always new as imagination, she found the dramatic climate romantic by convention as the monsoon lay a long siege to the house and everything else within its purview.

That house processed Nature, there is no doubt about it. It did it on the fringes in the beginning but later on, it was inside, like a regular rhythm, a lamentation of the wind before something went kaput, turning the house into a museum of experiences in a matter of thirty days. It was deep as dark outside, at the corners of the house. The corner light outside that made salvation a fascinating proposition was the first casualty. After that a bird, wanted in hell, perched on top of it and kept us awake most nights. After working tirelessly for years, one by one, the old droning fans suddenly started reaching the end of their careers. The cooler joined them in afterlife not long after. The mixie chose its ending in the following week. We had found it in a bed box and buried it back quietly, hoping that MIL would not need it anytime too soon. The TV became indifferent to our need for entertainment and went away to take on infinity. The tube lights, in great humility, flickered on for as long as they could. The nihilistic fridge was the second last one, going down without a fight. At least the grinding stone had the ball to fall and then break. At the end, it was a bolt of chilling lightning that first lashed, then bombed the house, as a result of which, the last thing to go off, one day before MIL's return, was the transformer. When we woke up in the morning, we were thankful to God that we still wore our breaths. We looked at the house from outside; it was hanging together by a thread. We had been made poor in no time. By no means, was that house meant for a good start in life. As soon as MIL returned, she made us sit outside and immediately the house was reconciled to its sole inmate.

The lights flickered back on. The fans were resurrected to their droning. The fridge chugged back to life. I don't know about the mixie in the bed box but the grinding stone put itself back together. The bolt of lightning withdrew itself from the transformer and went flying back into the disappearing storm clouds. The grass grew back long and lustrous. The light at the corner at night found its current. It was the best make-believe return to normality that I have ever seen. I was mysteriously raised in my childhood and so was Kaia and so was MIL and so are numerous other people but I can swear that when I see the frontline of the supernatural then that was what it was. The house had the dimensions of a sepia frame that needed the touch of the priesthood. There the endangered fetus was one step away from beyond. You can put your heart into work or into education or into marriage and home but the penalties of angry abuse do not result from the functioning of a thing called life but from the convulsions of hell with traces of aberration as the first signs. That dramatized idleness of one and a half months was an example. It would dog us for a few more months until a direct attack.

12.
Pop culture stuff

*T*he white-hot days of June were over. The rains in Rohini seemed like a revolution. They never seemed to come to an end. It was pop-culture stuff to stand in either balcony and listen to its music and song. There is something about rain that puts everything into retro mode. I don't know if the unborn feel it but it sure feels like the world is just beginning before it gets worse and worse and it seems the world is ending. The unborn can get impatient but ours was not yet in that stage to express anything. We walk-refreshed it every day, walking to feel the thin *drizzle* and damp air, the humid heat of the pavements in the *dazzling* sun, the passionate evenings, walking to coexist like smiles, one in the shadow of another's hot clinging clothes, walking to the end of the rain, walking to the end of humanity, walking to the beginning of the rain, walking to the beginning of humanity, walking in and out of storms, sometimes feeling like a family and sometimes not feeling like a family, walking until we ourselves felt kinda reborn and then sometimes unborn. I felt the lure of the balcony and turned the rain to my advantage. There were honest abandoned mud heaps all along the roads. Aren't people sometimes like that? In the comfort of a rainbow, between spells of the sovereign rain, I collected some with love's outreach in polybags for the new flowerpots I had lined the balcony with. For further interpretation, I put stolen, plucked and bought plants into the earth so befriended. Aren't souls like that? It is the soul which shows, thrives, grows, flowers, fruits, seeds, leaves, shoots and roots.

The earth remains in its place. Brown, yellow, black, white, solid, porous, rich, dry, watery and rocky. No wonder the priest says dust to dust ashes to ashes. When the soul leaves, the earth remains. It needs to be prepared for the next soul. Or souls. Though no one knows its past. The codes of transfer are also not physical. It is like a promise that is a word. It is spoken and heard and for years you know it. It could spell the birth and life of a nation or it could be the birth and life of a baby. Children are the souls of their parents. They are the morning and the evening of their days. Rain is fun. Flower pots are a hobby. A partner for life is the earth. Life is revolution. You can do a great job with whatever you have got. Just be creative. Never be bored. A beautiful world was born out of a problem. Be tough. You are right if you have not done any wrong. Teachers are not always people. A flower pot can be one. Rain can be another. Marriage is an education. Just look and you will walk beyond the limitless.

13.

The world would be him

Kaia was a bubble beauty by now. Her bubble had a life of its own, a career of its own, threateningly becoming more and more public, working in all grace as well as comic excellence. It needed constant tempering with larger clothes and more and more food and care and love and scratching and rubbing of heels. It was possible to know and feel the world inside the bubble. I felt the power of that in the stillness of the morning, evening or night hours, how it sought freedom, moving, turning, going about its revolutions, conscious of me trying to understand its ways. It put us on a quest, to change attitudes, to seek faith, to accept the simplicity of love with all its flaws, for the right training to make me a man from my incompleteness to train my successor to grow up to be a *Daniel* among the lions, to never abandon family and home, to keep love uncomplicated, to always have the confidence to face real life, to give him or her a sibling, to get everything right, to never lie, steal, cheat, beat and abuse, to never get cornered, to always provide, to always progress, to make this body a human temple, to be like Israel, a promised nation of sojourners. All this I believed was in the nature of becoming a father. There was a sort of future in some of those things.

Females belong to the future and only they follow the change patterns of the universe. I also love what they do with life and approached Kaia's body as if invited to a new dream, learning on the way about new and unfamiliar states of introversion which she launched from time to time, borrowing hours and hours. My heart was always present whether I was there or not, trying to speak the language of a creative being and experiencing every day as a genesis day. But actually, it was The Creator who was doing His God Stuff and it was His Word Voice, the one, within her, was listening to. I was not the first and the last father but it was a privilege to attend. The whole world became him. We needed just a whisper to call out to him in his deep inner silence and he leaped. He didn't mind the frequent change of names, though. A rose by any other name, you would say, but I say the whole life of a rose can be summed up in its fragrance and the whole life of its fragrance in its name. The fragrance is the character and the character has a name. Hence, the name is important. I had his name, caught off a dream which I had been swaying on, for some time.

I was a family-away by about two months.

14.
In for a day

The night around a mother is a sign that a boy is on the way. The inspired area for his arrival becomes his home. Everything else becomes work. Borne on the aching back of love, Kaia was getting to show the signs that she was carrying a boy. She was not capable of springing a surprise on me. And if she were, it would not be one for my heart of love, anyway. I had received a father's training from my father to bring up a boy or a girl. It was a boy because the makeup didn't work anymore on Kaia. In the meanwhile, my birthday bouquets began to bloom in a couple of cards, one from Rita and the viceroy and the other from her. The city was not going to pass me by without a celebration. That day I put aside my colorless work rags since Kaia whom colors met regularly, took me out for shopping for some. To keep passion afresh, I say, submit to a woman. I was like an infant out in a color haze. Kaia changed me in a day. You can tell, when a man changes. It's the outer wear. A woman's changes may only be guessed; the innerwear is only a known clue. I could take on the heat of a thousand summers with my white shirts but with my colorful shirts, questioning eyes made my world so conscious. Anyway, clothes are the skin of a mood; an invented tissue to hide or release the creature's appeal. Since my own annual skin during the winters comprised blazers, coats and suits only, Kaia made me equal to the rest of humanity by presenting me with a couple of sweaters too; one gave me the language of a new look and the other was quite the opposite or let me be kind and say that it only separated my personal from outer spaces, so thick it was and the warmest thing under the winter's dew. However, possessed with the knowledge of my need, she gifted me a Raymond's coat and trousers for Christmas. Thus, gift inured, I was controlled and held in place, however, I failed to present her with anything out of the economy of my heart.

15.

A home to decorate

O n our second Christmas, I had a home to decorate. Even as a child, I had always seen Christmas in all its transformative ranges. Vacation influenced a large part of it, no doubt, and I was accustomed to a month of it as a student. B-30 walls were white like nappies. And bare; it is such great knowledge, this bareness. But around Christmas, even they sought to be decorated, at least externally; the bareness of a wall can never be taken away. So, the house took on a temporary form of common decorativeness, a vitality akin to clothes, gifts and cakes. Christmas dinner was a free deal from MIL. The old chimes in her home gave all her guests love, faith, hope and joy that each one of them would always receive their fair share of pulao and korma and kebabs and fried fish and pork and chicken and even paneer. People felt important as soon as they sat at her dining table because she was a radical hostess. She took no time to connect you to the serving end of her ladle. It was like a magic wand with *witch* she touched you and made you feel free. Food was an idea that never stopped taking a public shape in her house, occasion or no occasion. It was there I discovered that a mother and a mother-in-law's food has a productive and a reproductive edge to it. You can seek the best cuisines in the biggest ranks of culinary five stars but your wife will not conceive. It happens when you return and are fed by either the mother or the mother-in-law. The label 'fertile marriage' has nothing to do with feminine or bearded masculinity. Cooking is a very moral discharge of duties and within the uncontradictory bounds of morality (because some people take pornographic pleasure in cooking); it is greater than any other art. My mother and my mother-in-law were unsung heroines of this art.

Hell is neither early nor late in our lives because it is always following us around. Hell is a secret which the devil keeps from us whether we sin or not. My wife looked like a pregnant nymph and got fits of fatigue and hunger and cravings and storytelling and backache and cramps and tightness and fright and negativity and anxiety and repulsion and cold feet but not shyness. She kept me awake at different times of the day, when at home, on holidays and at night always, to participate in involuntary acts that took care of any of the previously listed problems. Directions from her international sister comprised, besides phone calls and cards, a book on the very subject which more than her, I read. One evening, when we were at MIL's, she expressed a strong urge to have an ice-cream. Dhakka Colony partnered with a location called Vijay Nagar and that is where I took her. I am an observer of behaviors of humans, animals, birds, insects, plants, air, water, earth, sky, clouds, space, planes, helicopters, UFOs, spirits, angels, demons and what have you! and there I saw this hell's minister, pretending to be a bull, with horns as straight as Kaia's moral record.

They looked very scary as he approached us closer and closer while Kaia's belly lawfully protruded in every direction, as she swayed from side to side, enjoying an ice cream and meeting a fellow from either her college or the neighborhood or both while I tried to survive shyness due to such an exposure, since the eyes of every passerby became friends with her growing size. Also the coming attack and its object were in opposite directions, I had to keep one eye on the pregnant civilization and the other on the forces of destruction but didn't know what to do until the bull's horns were inches away from the two precious lives, one within another. My vison recombined the world into a single image and I distinguished myself, featuring forever as a hero in antiquity, by holding with one hand Kaia, who with unmatched pleasure did not only not let go of the ice-cream but was totally unaware of what was going on until she saw what my other arm was holding and my foot kicking, which when she did, she began to scream at the top of her voice, the ice-cream still tightly secure in her small fist, upon which the beast made its escape.

II
Redemption

1.
Present tense has a reputation to maintain

November 2016

I remain a robin on storm-watch. However, now my other biggest concern is trying to stay out of the erotic furnaces of the flesh. I have aged indiscreetly, reaching an unambiguous age from which there is no return and yet I am always a first-time man, ploughing my eyes of years through anytime, anyplace women. Kaia needs no introduction but now she is a greater love producer with bigger wallflower eyes, finer sugar fingers, and sweeter soundtracks in her skin that serve enchantments like never before. Diaz and Deb are human glue, rubbed in with love.

Inferring from the shadows at 3.15 am, it seems the sun has been on the rope all night. A lot of wind has accumulated at top end. Time for meeting God until a sunrise can be compiled. God moves the spheres. Today there is a hole in earth's miles. It's called holiday. Only Kaia has office. Tradition is a good direction for growing and Deb and Diaz haven't disappointed us. They answer all the cruelty I have shown them ever with hugs and kisses. They are predecessors of light and on inflated floors of a mall they are walking arm in arm with me before making me experience a money holocaust. After looking into windows of abundance, we enter the thresholds of one and Deb buys bliss but Diaz keeps the spending minimum so I get to keep my fart. While daylight is still the theme, we land up at McDonald's because I am not pledged to extravagant eating today. I send Diaz, our Bruce Wayne, and escorted by him, Kaia comes to us out of a very chic dusk and we merge our energies in laughter and fun.

Days of sad streets for Jonah as he paces about outside a Bareilly hospital, praying for his father's recovery. Sunny, my brother-in-law, is clawing through the limbo of an operation. The righteous rush is long gone from him since his wife's death in 2015 and he lies there in a miracle vacuum, listening to the drip. And yet he is not a mere mistake of the dust. Soon, he will be off to Heaven on the stellar tail of some doodle from infinity, escaping through zones of delirious dragons fighting for his soul. The hand of deep fear is also inches away from Kaia. The afternoon rises into a lavish lunch with Undo Bhai and Lola. The former is a blissful beast, always feeding alone as in a herd. The latter devours even the fish heads with reptilian cheer while in her wheelchair slouches MIL, catching and feeding on unbaked snails from a fitful dreaming inventory. It is not hard to age when children reach the cusp of responsible adulthood. Diaz is now doing internship. Kaia carries the sunrise into midnight waiting for him when he has to work even on weekends. When he comes, he joins her in pressing my feet and hands and then hers. His continuous boyish smile is the essence of his simplicity.

I am the only waking part and the first possessor of the morning. Driving to Khandsa to get the week's supplies is an exercise in solitude on the inky road, cast in the shadow of waking ravens. The hard designs of night are still fresh on their wings. Breakthroughs are granted by the Father of Immortality, the unending God. So we take the rosebud drying Book and head for church to take the cosmic pills of peace and healing and success and happiness. MIL's skin is parchment dry. It needs wild spirits of heat from atoms of fire. Kaia and Lola massage her with pork fat they purchased after church today. We are in the same room, Kaia and I but there is much distance between our eyes. Mine are shut on the bed and hers are open, the desk light shallow against their brightness. I can hear Diaz. He laughs and says *look he opens one eye*. We watch *Shining* while outside, a starless night applies itself.

I am rubbing dots of inky gloom from my eyes as I experience a deep awakening of the written ink in this house of higher winds. This inky gloom is yet to pick up pace as winter waits to become a perfect adult but I feel a presence of warm clothing over me already. It's half past rapture for Donald Trump in the US but the nation's ink is his greatest adversary. News is like a long party from morning till late night. The world is immobilised by US election results as a new day dawns there. Nirvana is happening on this side of the hemisphere too. The mythology makers of India cause a cash crash. Their working vision waited till Diwali was over but the red nosed members of Christmas wilt like ghosts before the assertive rats, now making their way out of the jungle towards the Bethlehem star. The latter will be ready some other day.

The moving ink from such a dense end of yesterday, dissolves into my creativity and I appear in an intense outdoor outfit. Stark blue trousers, black and white check shirt, brown shoes for the big picture today in school, that is, celebration of children's day. Kaia is not the only one laughing. In the lift, gentle Simba, our four-legged neighbour, looks away. Kaia says *bye Sheeba* and thereafter her ensuing laughter invades me with pleasure.

Lord of the bed gets us out of it. I follow Kaia to her bank, in defence of peace, to deposit her demonetised currency. Fear of money gets people into long queues. Everyone is waiting on the edge of a miracle. Black and grey and white personalities, talking about a new future. The future is only a serpent biting its own tail. Back at home at breakfast, we turn into food, love, jokes and laughter partisans. Diaz and Kaia indulge in hugs and kisses like an inseparable planet and its satellite. It's a dream day for Kaia. I work the whole day, making dinner at the end. She exercises her teeth in a smile until it turns inky after dinner. In bed, it is buried down in a galaxy, erased by my own twinkle. Her eye is the place where suns rise and set.

Repetitive first meal of joy, laughter at Kaia's antics and then work invades fun and tires Kaia and her mood has an ink effect on ours. Diaz reacts to it and the hugging and kissing stop. Both look miserable with undercurrents of surrender. Deb serves us fruit juice and sweet corn. Kaia moves only in two directions. After household work, it's office files. I hit the sack early and don't know when she is in bed. Sleep refreshes my professional body but hers says only a feeble hello to mine.

After a day, Diaz and mum's energies catch each other again and are reconciled to regular hugging and kissing. Online shopping mitigates demonetisation and other woes I encounter in Khandsa but those only the sky knows. Kaia looks very hot, adjusting her feminine freshness with some fragrance. Uff! I am besieged by her night's heat. Love is never a struggle.

An invading force into the edgy darkness of 4.30 am. The building feels a quickening breakthrough of some sort. The undercurrents of Nature giving birth to rodents. Entering from his dreams is Diaz, roused by the day-breaking earthquake, his head full of the soft shadows of inky sleep. I only give him a sentence-long smile, looking up from the mythical methi, diverting me for two days now from my transformative ink of creativity, at the still shaking chandeliers and the fans as if they are in a dance club. Later he mimics my action, comparing it to Billy in *Predator*.

I am extracting a birthday this month. At least once in the year we need it. My final hair are grey now and deafening about my ears and I must hack into them myself with a razor. I outline my body in the Nehru jacket, Kaia has gifted me. Sugar becomes more sweet when she sees me in the car and she keeps saying *you are looking nice, you are looking nice*. In the evening I bleed money and time, watching *Fantastic Beasts*. Moods are so off because of it that there are gaps of stars in the deep demon ink that cannot be called night. We visit F-5 with pizzas. A taste away is MIL, groaning because she is tangled somewhere in her sleep. We wade through the smell and surround her like a crowd of saints trying to produce miracles. Deborah now covers the scene with her adolescent wings. She is blade-faced over the way her fragile granny is being handled and dismisses our half hands and hearts and eyes and words and with sequels of her own celestial touches, helps MIL's sleep-blood flow again. Undo bhai had persevered to find me a card in the vanishing city's afternoon. I look at him with eye roses for presenting me an anniversary card on my birthday. The franchise spirit of devotion, Lola, makes coffee on popular demand. My special day of blessings ends with Diaz pressing my hands and feet. Tomorrow is working but tonight Venus is on tour and bed is an event.

A self-sun morning because Kaia is up before me. A snake of a day follows. MIL looks so fragile today that a butterfly could subvert her trip to the hospital. Lola, the keeper of her air and water stands aside, holding her papers etc. I have taken leave from labour and sit holding the steering. Kaia is an outpost of rushing-about, to see how best her mother can be transferred from her wheelchair into the middle seat. MIL is now only an old paper book mark from the tome she used to be once. She is only a husk and yet it is only Undo bhai, an agent of the winnowing wind, who *can do* it. He lifts and deposits her singlehandedly. Our fresh faces turn to ink, waiting for Doctor Ratz who finally casts his subterranean shadow on us and with his molehill gaze tries to understand MIL's symptoms, slapping her parchment cheek, chanting *naam batayein, naam batayein.* Everyone follows him into his room. On her stretcher is MIL, a mere abstraction covered with a white sheet. Serpentine crowds pass by, looking for new direction but MIL is in the way. I pull her closer but she, with incoherent and brief wailing, gets herself away and into the way of raining eyes. Kaia, Lola and Undo bhai come out and glide MIL through cold marble and tile corridors and then a cold steel and glass door and she slips under a line of cold silk light that scans her. We get back. There's fresh pace as we go through some shopping. Our day of happiness begins tomorrow but Kaia has a mother of smiles on her face. The house is full of light because of it. The table is crowded with guests because of it. Undo bhai and Lola are bound by it to hog and hug all the food and the fun. Only MIL is free in her wheelchair to drool, make sounds, oscillate and slump deeper and deeper into a place of faint stars, a place of candles in the path of God. A slack moon rises. Kaia has the energy of a snail but miracle is a movement of Deb's fingers deep in oil, running through Kaia's hair and Diaz's iron fingers locking around the ache in her feet whereas I am allowed to move tiredly into a working sleep.

Companion day to yesterday. We make the celebration greater, transcending to an epicure's revenge to what was served yesterday on which Undo bhai and Lola should descend but he is late and Kaia holds with him a council of culpability. It ends with penetrating words like *there is always some communication gap with you.* He dissembles, trying to add a degree of opposition with a usually stoic *no no.* She asks *weren't you told yesterday?* His tongue equivocates defencelessly with the usual *yea yea.* Lola is pleased with the persecution and with terrible ease proceeds to the table where she will meditate with a holy peacefulness on the fish. Consuming the bones is a passionate religious decree. She keeps up a frail praise till next day. After an interim gap, we all ascend to some distinguished dialogue on Skype with Rita and the viceroy. She is a judge, a discerner and a scorner but Kaia does not retreat from her jokes, in fact, the more she laughs at her, the more Kaia is united with her. 12.00 am. Time to be pursued by Diaz and Deb's affection and accommodate their healing kisses, hugs and wishes after which prosperity establishes itself. Kaia receives headphones and I receive woodland slippers from Diaz and a Van Heusen shirt from my wife. Deb feels condemned by all this show of prosperity by her brother and triumphantly says *I am broke.*

The long partying ends today at Forest Festivity in Leisure Valley. I am a friend of nature but this simulation with life-size animal heads, pressing plastic deformities, sticking out of pressing plastic foliage, produces a pressing melancholy. Perhaps only the waiters, in green safari suits, are trying to read nature with all that standing and staring. The place is blasphemously subverted by frail and beautiful women with extremes of bodies that belong in a heated rainforest. Not cutting character, my eyes hunt them down subtly in the limited holdings of the place. My eyes pick out taste from so much distaste. Kaia is contemplating on me. I cannot remain hidden from her very long, so I get back to the food and mock-tails. Outside, Deb shoots a video of Kaia. Her face, in the deep recesses of her fur hood, is a creature peering out of a soft white cloud. We are transferring ourselves to the dark and sombre world of F-5 with felicity stars but also some food. Undo bhai is habitually happy, spiralling pathless with meaningless phone calls or typing his quarter book of happiness, of recipes, medical tips and just plain trivia on Rita's defunct laptop or watching the numbing display of electricity on the blank TV screen since cable has been cut or secretly quickening himself with hard rock desi sharab. In the other bedroom under the watchful eye of Lola, secretly thanking the coming sorrow that will free her, MIL is on a pathless spiral, dreaming of a floral sun in afterlife. Dan and Deb divide up the play with their granny's grave body. We postpone smiles while helping to finish the ice-cream but all the way back, are crushed by laughter. It is made more chaotic by my sorry fart that does not also escape Deb's mobile camera. In bed I locate Kaia's homely bosom, headquarters of silk, and forget the bush party prey. Love is a series of persons. One experience is always different from another.

The sun sets in lesser skins as I wait at the metro and yet holding my skin in place are the ghazals when Kaia appears in the disguise of a far look. F-5 has begun to drift away, anyway. Undo bhai is on street practice to Nicholson graveyard and also to look for MIL's grave. He casts a short shadow on the doorstep and exclaims *good news! Found her grave!* That is, the one she had booked for her own humble day of dust when long ago FIL was descending into his own. Kaia is happy as dove's fart, offering him sweets and all but when I point out the irony, she unites her epileptic laughter with his full-throated one.

2.
Starless Zodiac

*T*his morning is totally spent by the transformative dots of a dense fog when I set out for school but a fine cruel sun has parted it by the afternoon and as I turn in the direction of many winds around a bend that fits the dusty road after Wazirabad red light, it reveals a wind wearing silhouette on a different sail. Around its stage of loneliness, below its bowed head, there is a crowd with blankness condensed deep into the furrows of their faces; they have been standing there for hours and looking up at its inseparability from the vastness of a suicidal end. I come to a body-stop with a jerk but when I start again, time gets ahead of me and after that every day that tree of despair at that bend in the road, springs out at me with a grief that does not seem to come to an end. I spend hours and hours of heart and soul with Kaia but only an encounter with Sam would set me free from this ulcer of the soul.

Chaos is orbiting around the earth that is why when I am embroidering my woman's borders with my eyes, her mood goes off suddenly. She is watching *Dead Poet's Society* while finishing dinner on the sofa and gets up and turns to me and says *when you will come on Saturday from school, then I will also not sit with you at lunch.*

Her mood enables a certain loneliness but there's been no fog since Saturday. Night remains a prosaic statement. No releases. Cannot stand this accretion in the elect sacs.

Hell's definition is not necessary. God is necessary. Shadows are enclosing MIL gradually. It's a one way trip from now on. A religious end is necessary. On request from Kaia, the padre comes and ministers the Holy Elements to her. Four mad days of the school's annual day are over. Normal existence is necessary. Let us burn the future completely tonight. Love is necessary.

We rise from our ashes. Kaia visits MIL, morning and evening. The occult orbits around Christmas. A red nosed light is inching ever so close. The Christmas tree, a winter king, reigns supreme in all the profane worlds. We take out ours. Only the sparkle of God is missing, otherwise all else is a glittering mingle of decorations, lights and music. I would rather put my life in a candle, beating about the great darkness descending on us. A bowl of peace and goodwill should suffice for now.

The hurrying sun goes and we lose ourselves in a shopping and eating-out limbo on Christmas Eve. I love females, extracted from centuries of feminine moments, for what they do with life. Only they can add that extra layer of light and longer fire to such a Gotham's dark night as this one.

Morning touches me before it does anyone else and I see the partial star of Christmas rising among the young stars. There is a new world in our dreams and the rest of the day in our imagination. Lola is a bearer of glory from the church with us. Undo bhai is suspended over a gap in the planet where MIL is headed before the year is out.

Part of the sun is immersed into the horizon by the time both finish having lunch at our place by turns. I refused being colonised long ago by the British. Besides I have roots of tiredness going long and deep which my feet only know from and to where. Hence, I am in bed but Lola is guffawing with Rita and the viceroy on Skype while I am experiencing sleep interference due to it. By night I need whispers of inner silence but the voice I hear at bedtime is the singing voice of life, a whole voice of dreams. Kaia's flannel voice is now doing her turn at Skype.

Christmas colours are getting exhausted. The land is moving faster under our feet. We are not the only ones *not* on the world's peaceful side. Jonah has texted that their dad is drifting towards the inevitable. Death is preparing her laces.

A stage is required to show Undo bhai's strange behaviour now a days. It ranges from don't do to can't do to won't do. With her aging stable claws, Lola Florence Nightingale alone cooks, alone washes, alone cleans and alone holds MIL through the day and beyond the night. *You will go Ma*, she whispers, *only when I will say so*. I have wonder eyes for Kaia's thunder. With what speed she cooks for her mother's nurse and delivers the food and goes to office but tonight, when the darkness is only a mile deep, she is called down by Lola. The patient has put on a very deathly colour and is awash with infinite fluids oozing out while Undo bhai has locked himself inside his self-indulgent night, tilting with cheap country-made alcohol. Together the two women rub the pausing sky against the galaxy and only when the moon gets going again, does she return at the tail end of the inky night.

3.15 am. Lapwings are the eyes and the cries of the night, though there is no sunset or sunrise for them. I also detect a continuous hammering sound. Somewhere, someone is doing some work of eternity. After finishing kitchen work by 4.30, I am ink happy with the table tide of words and am well into my pages, recruiting new characters into the surging story while an old one, namely, Sunny goes on the ventilator. A star way is opening for him. An episode will cease soon. This pulls some gloom into the story but by the laws of winter sunrise, I am, as I have said before, the first possessor of light. Today, Undo bhai has finally done a *cando* thing and calls a doctor. The air glows around his head and it pleases Kaia to no end. At night, the mirror feels creative as she adjusts my fur cap on her head before sitting and working on her files. I watch her from the bed. Happiness is want getting longer and bigger in the skin's desert of beauty. In deep winter, she is the woman with the right mix of summer. I want the night but Deb destroys the possibility by flashing her mobile camera to click pictures of her mother.

The sun is in conflict with its sunshine. Only one of them can be seen alternately. God Himself is squeezing the air so tightly around MIL that she should soon achieve a breakthrough to hell. Her breathing is a precipitating swamp sound of a sorrowful struggle to either live or die but whichever it is, Undo bhai and Lola are on either side of her, trying to help her do it faster while Deb is grappling with the phenomenon of existence with words and touch of love. Kaia asks me at the metro station, teary eyed, *is she gone?* and is on the edge of a heartbreak at the sight of the dried up fountain of crumpled ink that used to be her mother. In the entire history of fists, hers must be the tightest in hysterical frustration at this moment. Then suddenly the doors of the house announce themselves by opening and shutting and then those of an ambulance and then those of the Emergency ward and then those of the ICU and then those of life because there in the ICU, in no time, MIL escapes into dust. Miracle of close vicinity, Dougs are the first to be with us. Undo bhai opens up like a ruined book of tears but someone puts an arm around him and he shuts it. It is difficult to believe that inside the ICU, there were human beings, the way the strutting staff, wrapped and covered and sheathed from head to toe in skill, are dismantling the dead, including MIL. Strangely, I don't remember seeing blood. These people achieve so much each day, serving death to a conscious, throbbing, intelligent city! Kaia makes no shadow. *I want to be by my mother's side in the mortuary* she says but while some of my waking ends are still active, I bring her home by midnight. Our faces have turned to muddy earth and the night surrounds us like the skin of the vacuumed dead.

The only colour we meet are all the final flowers we buy from old Gurgaon. MIL's body, a frail white candle, is on a cot. Dr. Nero transforms into a self-appointed evangelist, preaching salvation. I encourage him to speak a few words of comfort. He does so but the prayer is a conversion prayer again. The British arrive and the air is refreshed as they sweep everyone and everything with their London gaze. The candle-crossed room brightens up. The flowers look up. Even the deceased resurfaces briefly from the depths of floral and artificial fragrance. The hearse takes the corpse road with MIL's time-box.

At the cemetery, the walk of death is led by the padre. I am photographing the undisturbed vegetation rising out of the earth and the inscriptions, infiltrating the earth. We leave when MIL is united with the last of the candles with the day's end on top, long into the dusk. The last night of the year does not seem to pass us by. Death is rest but we are restless.

3.
Hazing

*T*he year is out like a worn out infant. Memorial service committee swings into action. By 11.30 pm, death has struck again with former high frequency. Jonah calls and says *papa is no more* and with that the two children graduate to becoming orphans on New Year's Day today. Their mother, Aru my sister, had her humble day of dust in 2015. After Rita and the viceroy leave for their five star hotel, Kaia's eyes are the only lights in the room.

Laughter is a limited matter these days but Diaz must laugh. Even the birds have chosen this day to chirp. It's his birthday today. He becomes simple as an infant with all the wishes, hugs, kisses and gifts. A little celebration in the evening returns him to childhood days even though today he is such a health-being. His biceps are growing. His chest is expanding. His beard is shapeless. His hair unruly. His voice deep. His angst terrible. His frown darkest. His silence mysterious. His love choking. His kisses rough. His embraces bear-hugs. His energy undiminishing. His habits disgusting. His feet, socks and shoes smelly. His clothes everywhere. His manners funny. His punctuality, dedication and sincerity models. His cupboard messy. His jokes hilarious. His comings, goings, mobile messages, calls all riddles. Rita calls to wish him. Her conversation is like wine. The person who is totally drunk on it, is Kaia. I am drunk on her and when the dawn is in our nest, I am in her.

The story of birthday returns. It's Deborah's today, beginning on a damp note. MIL's memorial service is at 4.00 pm in the church. Dididi and Sully arrive. Rita reads her eulogy, trembling and choking. Back at home we have dinner. Sam, Dididi's driver, says a prayer! Rita keeps looking at my Dididi and what does she see there? Oh my Dididi, she has a persona of ageless stories and culture and life and special colours and exploration and focus and stability and perspective and comforting oils and idealism and earth's experience and wisdom and motivated thinking and innovation and comfort and compassion and unmapped memories and she has astonishing mastery over kitchen and she can stabilise suffering trees and she has a pervasive look of grey wilderness in her hair that prevents her from getting a look of the year and in her episode voice she gives ongoing reviews that can cause an ear overload, and incremental tiredness and she has an aspect of pure mind in her face for there is no mask there and laser charged surgical sharp eyes that also look far and a love for God so deep that He will need her presence in His courts and unmapped hope in the quintessence of comedy in everything. Rita cannot help but say that her voice is soothing and her face young. A movement is finally generated and the British are seen off and we land up at F-5. Lola with her long dragon bones is pulling out MIL's old and new clothes from the shelves and packing them up in MIL's suitcases to carry off to Bangalore next day. Back on our bed, we all cramp the sunset in our bedroom with Diaz and Deb on either side of Dididi, dividing the moments between them and telling them about our childhood's irrecoverable worlds in Hategrah. Her word rain will not end anytime soon but tomorrow the dust waits to swell up in our path of darkness to that lost world and so I labour out of her word swamp. Kaia is asleep like a new immortal but for me, a million distances of sleep already vanish as soon as I lie down beside her. The alarm rings but before the beginning of light, I want some more night.

Surrender to morning at last and we are propelled onto our journey. The country roads begin to close in on us as we take one to Hategarh, my roots country. Distances have towns in them but this one is farthest from Providence. It is an outpost of the demons of the north. The day is on a better display from my seat next to Sam who now I know is a pastor. Light rushes past us into the afternoon and we follow it through the wandering works of God and man as silence has not got any chance to respond to Dididi ever since we began and so the resulting streets have confused Sam very badly. We keep asking for the address and he keeps driving into the despairing horizon but after several attempts of repositioning the miles and smiles, we reach Hategarh. Our long trip faces are indistinguishable from the dark but time is not expensive here. My camera is rolling. There should be a rooftop moon but when Jonah comes out to open the gate for us, it disappears into his ecliptic hair, long as hell's weed, swallowing up light and all its sources. Dona, a definite case of loneliness in pale health, is like a slight interlude in all that hair darkness. He takes great care, not allowing her to stray out of it but the fiction of this house has spun out of control. Sam senses the backstage world of an older drama here. We make way through parents of shadows into the house and discover that the only choice for some dinner lies outside. Like buyers of the night, Sunny, Sam and I, go out to the crossing of faces and eyes and buy food and some other stuff for the morning. Sam says the grace and it either makes or finds an opening for angels to descend from their millennia of light into the hairy dark house. After dinner, the night meters are on but God's gloom is as yet limited. I search for a bathroom. The only usable one is in the vicinity of a candle, many house lights away. As I lower my haunches into the shadows, the window behind gets onto my skin's edge and when it begins to crawl, I rush out. Night releases its hair long into our conversation and gradually our skins part into the skins of the parts of a smile. There is some pooled laughter for the two children but that is later. It is a night's night and Jonah's smile makes nothingness of the light and if he wants to say something, it will have to be tomorrow for behind half his hair is a sunrise and we must all sleep now. Sam is already elevated over a snoring abyss. An insomniac mobile's light labours through either Jonah or Dona's quilt. A whale-sized moth covers the dining room light but the psalms, playing on my laptop, see us through the remaining night.

After a few hours, God puts the morning on the house but imagination conjures up the past in the semi darkness of what is now the predecessor of a kitchen. There are terribly unusable quantities of sugar, salt, flour, spices, oil etc. After breakfast, the day has a passing swiftness to it. Sam is a bearer of supernatural tales. They are as humorous and interesting but also as scary as cobra or spitting spirit rivers of lost afterlife with venomous turns and twists. A lot of time goes in the sun in the churchyard. The wall meddles with the grass that is so tall on either side that possibly it doesn't want any more growth. A butterfly flying backwards comes out of it and I see I am standing on the graves of my loved ones in some Picasso form or another inside them. I am saying this in the hearing of bees that we are always looking for the substance of immortality but if the mind can piece together the day in its declining voltage then we consider it enough. The day tears thinly and two people emerge out of it. One is Jonah and Dona's elder phoophee, frail as the skin of an onion and her daughter, transparent as the same and sends a million breathings through Sully's chest per second. Feather inspiration gets him excited in no time. He wants to peel off the beautiful with one constant question *how are you so fair?* Our initial limbos of monologues build up to word stairways that we hope will help the two orphans rise out of the deranged spirals of abysmal gravities but there is no hope. I take God's easy name. There is a pause in the flowing light as the very mother of wandering nights takes a holiday from everywhere else and comes and stands where the camera is resting on stacks of God's ink and the gadget comes under some sort of siege because it stops recording. Jonah has begun to speak, switching on a light in his personal worlds for us to see them better. There are personal snake skins with gods reborn as wrinkled bugs crawling through them and sunrises over no earths and poetry stranded in the music of tears and I have to switch off the camera because it just won't record any of it. Sully is seeking a last smile from the phoophee's daughter but her lily eyes are beginning to get tangled in the sunset and they decide to leave. There is dust in the wind's shadow as they do but Sam delivers a fire-breathing prayer over it all and a face like God's appears and demons dash out through paper doors and we are mended even physically. My headache is gone and Dididi's wheezing and cough stop. Jonah is still way down and his visage is the hairy sunset and inside that large brown shawl of his, he has become an outline of silence, going through some cave moments. By dinner Sam has a divine hold on me and makes me say the grace. Power outage plunges the house into a Rowling night. I peer outside to see who the night is tonight but it is just another country night. A wand of light from some fair star plays sequel to electricity. However, if you are searching for fear, then step into the back courtyard where winnowing rats are busy separating stellar remains of fallen angels' husks.

At 4 am the alarm rings followed by the song of a fowl. The tea fills the gap until others wake up. I am aware of hallucinations but the water shortage is real. A mug of water is enough for my ablutions. My first interaction with a candle in a long time takes place. Dididi is on one side of it and the kitchen on the other. We can have a good thousand starts but it always comes to this. The bags are packed. Our visit has reached its crumpled end. The two nobody's children sit up in their crumpled bed and witness it. I am not the man here and plead with Sam to pray and my epiphany is a hole in the hair and a change of words overcomes me or let me say that the words coming out of my mouth don't own me and with them my tears come out in person. I say to both *you are our spiritual children and this is not the end but a new*

79

beginning. Thus made capable of seeing our way, we get out. Jonah and Dona, mere outlines, come to the gate and once it closes, the house achieves a tonal universality with the sentient ink around it and we too are damn well on a flying road that cannot be overtaken by Jonah's long hair if Sam drives us in the right direction and speed. Dididi has no choice but to begin speaking. The journey through Bewar is not an idiot's tour. The way is fixed and nonstop through the dawn, lies a gradual sunrise in the horizon's skin. By the time we hit the capital, it is twelve.

We stop at Noida, Sully's sister's home but I am only a Metro away from home. I am on a supernatural course anyway. The road will restart for Dididi and Sully in the evening. Deb, our healing host, in syllables of smiles and angel phrases of welcome, opens the door. I bury some of my journey dust in all the hugs I receive but I have to give one to Rita, dressed in the latest timeline fashion and sitting like the Sphinx on tons of meditation! Kaia, who is daily pretty is looking beautiful. She intervenes with an offer of methi and mushroom gravies but Rita says *let me have some intelligent conversation* and I open the Pandora of my experiences until Diaz's addictive build shows up in the doorway. I stand and welcome him and that does not go unnoticed and everyone feels that I have had an encounter with The Awesome. In fact, Deb suspects if I am her copyrighted dad and asks three questions to ascertain if I am or not. A saint has been initiated in me. I announce we will have a prayer meeting with Dougs and Jensens. Rita crosses herself and says *hallelujah* with a gothic smile and Kaia adds subtitles to her disbelief. Wow she says *I cannot believe it! What has happened to your father!!* And I wonder why salvation is never nearest! I put on my party skins because my late FIL's relatives show up. They are a super species. There is one among them unexplored, authentic young find with spring on her lips and its floral gold on the rest of her. Such things exist, I know now. She is quite outside the latitudes of anyone's dreams. Where is she from? I find out later. She works in Vancouver. She is quite a singalong; she is. Before the party reaches the last splurges, I discover the Vancouver girl in the kitchen, helping, serving, clearing, cleaning and washing. She is immediately my favourite and I want her as my daughter-in-law. She has what it takes to be family. She is the kind who will lift the world from wherever it is and I can't know the whole thing but I want to hold her babies in my arms. Why does Diaz have such a serious look on his face? It is time for them to go and the Vancouver girl plants a condensed flower kiss, a fantasy of butterflies, on my cheek. Before hitting the sack, in my newfound capacity, and this is on script time, I bring everyone to pray by holding hands and look at Deborah and Diaz like Sam and say *pray*! And Deb does and then Diaz does and then Kaia does and lastly I do. Rita crosses herself and I think she is being facetious with that gothic smile of hers but the viceroy assures me that she is not and then Undo bhai and Rita hug and both weep bitterly and forgive each other but future is budgeted time and they quickly sit in their five star hotel car and leave for their five star hotel. All pieces work wonderfully once set. Love has been in deficit. I have access to it again and Kaia tonight is as free as a street and I am a pioneer.

Winter gets its first warning to wear down with Lohri today. Sleep circumvents the alarm. I have discovered that there are several categories of me. God's frontiers converge on one in the morning and I worships Him. After that, blessings become work. Rita thinks Undo bhai is preparing for a new uncertain start by getting drunk but everyone knows it has an old hold on him. She asks to check on him. Fun always just works with her. Akhtari, their maid exercises her unique advantage and great capacity to take away a lot of stuff from F-5. Pastor Sam confirms he will be here on 21st with a miracle. Dougs and Jensens have confirmed they will get to the miracle. The other category needs a criminal amount of love and I make Kaia sit in my lap. Love is for long keeps but for now, together we experience the long fate of the night.

Kaia and I sit in bed always working towards a new end but tea is always present in it like an old beginning. The path to a new end is a mood. A grumbling. An argument. A fight. These keep things clear. And home is a place for them just as love has a place at home. So together we approach the wish to fight. She begins with a grumble about Diaz's job. I end her grumbling by grumbling at her for grumbling in the morning. Her lips get into a comical shape that says without moving that her mood has improved. Hence on her suggestion, wingless we rise into the city where according to my bone capacity, I drift along through the shopping until prospective tenants for F-5 begin calling her. After all, she is on the inheritance side of things now with her sister, and she condescends to change direction only then. She shows the house to one named Khan. A change has come over F-5. All the house lights are on to keep the adversaries of light out. Behind them all is Undo bhai with a ruined bent smile. The TV is flashing, going through the repetitions of the day. There is an outflow of clothes from cupboards and beds, tied up in huge pregnant bundles but a little bit of the house is still able to peep from here and there through the gaps. After dinner, we watch Nixon. Beauty's real business begins in bed. I am rewarded for loyally staying by Kaia's side.

Kaia invites Undo bhai for lunch. He is the remains of his former self. There are gaps in his face. Nights fill the two holes where his two eyes should be. Where is the smile that used to be a book, full of pages and writings? In fact, he has been eating darkness. It is still smeared around his mouth. There is a shadow at the bottom of his suns. He walks slightly behind his body, speaks in shrimp voice and when he eats, he lacks the inner feasting. He mourns his choices of the dos he didn't and the don'ts he did. His eyes are a barrier but I detect dried up river maps on the cheeks. The wind's roots are caught in the cold by the evening but the clouds are like lost sojourners so that a part of the firmament keeps passing. Want a little summer on the side but Kaia is a clamouring fairy. I make her sit beside me on a *modha* and from my hands outflows oil into her inky hair where they intersect the depths of the night and the freshness calms her down into a sleep.

Support the morning by getting up with it. Lifts are stuck. Have to take the steps all the way down. Evening comes up and brings Khan, the tenant, to sign the papers. He is a lawyer and a professor. In front of him, we are like information start-ups.

News dawn with Trump's inauguration. Kaia joins me. Sam has started a breakthrough in my life. After that the spectacular has just grown and made each day.

The new song has kept the transition going for so long. My best today still inspires the air and light to be rebuilt around me. But I am a lonely hope. I go to pick up Sam. The sky is in the wind around him as he steps out of the Metro. I am empty as a snail's shell but he fills it up with one hug. At home we minister and listen to him with our hearts on spiritual twigs and it is midnight before you know it. We hit the sack but Kaia cuts through the middle of the night with a knife and a grate, trying to make *gajar ka halwa*.

Sam and Diaz put the moon behind them and rise like the sun. They are in the kitchen and without training, try to find the means to make some tea. Sam says he could not sleep since madam was going around doing *khut khut khut* in the kitchen. Kaia exclaims *long is the happiness of the damn gajar ka halwaa over mine! It's not only drying up!!* After all the cooking is done, time parodies a film reel's 24 frames. Diaz calls. He has a growl or two in his voice. Deb says *he sounds like that on Kaia's phone*. Kaia rushes to get flowers. Deb lights candles. Jensens arrive. Undo bhai is all suited booted. Dougs follow. Fruit drinks and chips are served. We begin singing. Sam gives the sermon. Deb, Diaz and I pray. The camera rolls. Everyone joins hands. Sam is in the middle. Olive oil is poured. The children are dedicated. We say *hallelujah*. We eat. The relatives are seen off. We visit F-5. The camera rolls. Sam prays. I experience the power again. The woman in the neighbourhood screams. Sam mumbles a prayer. She quietens down. Undo bhai is wished good night. Diaz and Sam walk like friends. Kaia, Diaz and I present Sam cheques and cash. Deb gives him a pastry. Sam blesses us and then he leaves via some sky street to his home where sunset and sunrise straddle at the same time. Kaia and I leave night on the wayside and go into the sound and fury of sleep. Deb and Diaz carve out the work between them to clear the mess but not in the silence of creation but with the high metallic din of gods' meetings in the mythologies. Kaia's ancestors of sleep are sorry to be woken up thus and like a fairy owl, she wind walks on wing tip to the kitchen to make the midnight easier but they push her out and send her back into a dream lane. She is the existence of all the fun for them so they will mimic her next day.

Each moment stays a little longer in the slow choreography of each look. Undo bhai brings a substantial super-wealth of that in his face when he comes up to discuss his departure. I can see he consumed only a day's space and browsed only stars last night just because they are all free or at least that's what he says though information is always young on him but Kaia has the right to be still involved and offers him food. He is very thankful but eulogizes his nephew's wife. Kaia gives him money and then they reach that point I began with: the stuff of pause and flow, pause and flow; a choreography of emotions. It's a different labour for Undo bhai so he ends up comforting her with tears and a laugh and a few words and his yea yea and no no.

The neurons ease for us and for Undo bhai living under the rules of the consenting sisters who own F-5. He needs no past which only comprises time incorporated into mistakes. His life is a frontier of moving somewheres and someones. He fastens himself to nothing. He falls ill and Kaia comes early and brings him up and he experiences house and home, lying on the sofa and covered with a blanket and served hot and fresh food and everyone thinks he is just playing but I know he can get no acting role. He waves to me with that inverted still look of tight emotion, loose motion and vomit when I enter the house. Kaia and I interweave in sleep and when we wake up, she takes me down, saying *let's go and pack up his things or we will not be able to do anything tomorrow and send him off* even though he keeps saying *no no I will do it and yea yea I will do it.* He goes ahead of us to open the door and Kaia and I follow and there! It is a forever of disorder. Clothes and linen of every shape, description, kind, colour and age have come out of the pregnant bundles and they are populating the floor and some wait to escape as soon as the door is opened. Kaia looks at him in utter horror but the man says *no no* and when she says *what no no* he says *yea yea.* I pack everything into boxes and cartons and suitcases and bags and he and Kaia generate webs of silky praise around me. Next she sticks her nose into the fridge and cannot finish her sentence. How many destinies the man must have ended including MIL's with this approach to life. There is a lifetime of unopened vegetable packets, each with its own spawning ecosystem. I know now that poverty is an option. You have to book unpredictability with Undo bhai I tell Kaia. After some time, the love logos are back in her eyes and she brings him up food-hooked for some fresh meat.

Morning has been taught for the last six and a half decades to recognise what today is. A national cloud of rain darkens overhead. Kaia needs my face around again alongside. That's just what woman wants from her man and feeling like united bullies we go down to F-5. However, her company is always exciting and I'm speaking to her in English. She prefers it that way outdoors but I have to lower it slightly as a mark of respect to the society's Republic Day celebrations and it builds me thoughts to see the returning, amplified residents communicating the tricolour to everyone in some form or another on their faces, arms and person. Kaia and I repack Undo Bhai's personal bags while he is at the intersection of raining eyes behind a door. She whistles a midwife's tune all of a sudden as one of the hand bags gives birth to an amniotic sac full of *Santra Desi Sharab* bottles!! With much more than distance in her voice, she confronts him at breakfast upstairs *why are you drinking?* He gives her a wide-angle look and says *no no* and *yea yea* and adds *I do it out of loneliness.* Immediately Kaia shuts up but then I begin softly and gently and compassionately and chokingly and he listens to me with his heart's tears and laughter. He holds out his hand and I take it and then like an associate of God's government, I add *He is giving you chance after chance, so don't do it* and he agrees with *yea yea* and *no no.* With Undo bhai, one gets this feeling, as we go down to his taxi that one has been to this end before. The driver fits everything in the cab including Undo bhai but Undo bhai's path would always remain a guessed one and so we bid him farewell and off he goes and Kaia's sigh of relief is all over me. Now we have to sort out all the rubbish that Undo bhai couldn't take. Diaz calls her up and she says *he has a growl or two in his voice* and I say *he sounds like that on your phone.* After breakfast, he comes down and puts on this doing face like his mother and cleans the fridge in no time and takes off the curtains in no time and then he is gone and it begins to rain and first it is plain and simple, letting me share its vocals and that helps me hit the work real hard otherwise hard work takes the funny years out of you and soon enough the kitchen cupboards begin to look like new wood and then it begins to rain tigers and the tenant Khan comes with his friend, dragging endless trollies of polycarbonate suitcases that turn the roaring rain into butterfly print. MIL's room gets a brand based background but they have carried a conversation from the gate that has the story of F-5. It is posed as a question: *was the previous tenant a patient?* Kaia corrects him: *the previous patient was my mother.* Further union with work is renewed when Deb joins us but the day remains negative. The house has evolved into the diffused craziness of a badly cluttered character with rubbish bags and discarded stuff from the kitchen and cupboards and clothes and curtains and the rain is worrying us with its patience so I have to go and call the sweepers, a clutter of characters in their smug raincoats, who are busy like bad weather industry loading their rubbish vehicle with heaps of bags and declare that it's a holiday but as long as we are lost together, it doesn't matter. Anyway, every day is unequal so we go up and Deb orders pizzas and after that consistent are the hours of my sleep and Kaia's severe backache and Deb's healing massage.

It takes years to create our waste and in the name of the world we call it work. Morning is only an idea but we are up and about and down and out, heading towards F-5. The Republic's passionate buntings from yesterday lie trampled in the paths of where the rain has passed and where the people have. We take our maid with us and she wastes no time embracing as much waste as she can with the help of her people and today even the man-lot, the smug sweepers are the fast ones in taking away what no one will and then the F-5 maid comes and sweeps and mops the house and we turn and look at it, the way it had ever appeared and we turn and look at how it made us work to make it look tame and calm and at the end we again turn and look at how its soul returns and time will grow in it.

A liberated sunrise but just yet mind is not for me as Kaia and I go down to bring up all the waste *we* have separated for our own house. What a constant she is after that final round, bathing and dressing and getting after everyone to follow suit and to leave the house in time and then getting into a temper and screaming as Khan's friend is late and when he does finally come, the handing and taking over of F-5 is done and then I am off focus and take the wrong road and cause further delay and Kaia does not spare us a taste of her formula lecture, saying *you people are never late for a movie* but I think she is wrong as we have missed the opening of many movies and I need a way out of the big traffic jam but we fall silent. The jam finally clears and Diaz is my smooth navigator till Mandir Marg and as the redbrick building of St. Thomas's looms into view, I see what I already knew that we are not late because Mr Jensen is just getting out of his vehicle and then we see the others waiting in the sun and their names begin to run in my head as I park the car on the other side. A review of wife in the rear view mirror is needed but she has already gravitated into a lower emotion and is looking away so we get out, walk across and begin shaking hands, hugging and kissing as if on a debut business of live loving. The Laval family from Lucknow are here and led by Uncle Laval, the emperor of longevity, bent now so as to make it easy to be reached with a kiss but all along his spirit is always upright. Age is in his figure up to his eyelids but not in the rest of his eyes. They are still in their seeing years as his ears are in their listening years and his teeth are in their biting and chewing years and his mind is in its agile years and his voice is in its strong years and his love is still fresh with which he still admits me into his arms, remembering and calling my name! His son, my cousin, Remy views me from the top of his height but I will feel tall later alone. The day is on heat but inside the church it is cool. He has never been the one to go on a long journey of words. We are anyway poorly supplied with topics. I find myself attracted to the afterlife aura of expired names on the walls. I also find myself attracted to printed saris and kurta borders and their contents. While my camera is filling a few gaps, someone just floats in the padre. He is a little on the wrong side of perfect health, so the only thing that seems to hold him in the air is his infectious smile and happy words but he has a range of seriousness from explaining the order of the service to completing it around the baptism niche at the back where we all gather. My camera wants more of the face in the frames of the infant, her father, mother, Godmother, Godfather, the padre and his assistant but I say *use the zoom please* and it does but punishes me by blurring some pictures. Well, the quartet continues to exhibit great personal quality with the vows and the readings and the responses while the baby does its rounds between them as per the padre's instructions to it and then the afloat padre takes the little one in his arms, executes the final blessings and then still he hasn't had his landing. In fact, he beams all the more with life and light and love and laughter.

The crowd's face falls away from the baptism font, changing instantly from prayer to conversation, kissing and congratulations. Back in the sun there is a mixed exceptionality of aromas and I follow the nonvegetarian course and after locating it, holler to Diaz and we are in business with kebabs and chicken tikkas and cutlets until the rival estates lose out and everyone comes in and we all sit together as a praying pack ready for lunch but first the cake express arrives. A sad surging of wicked laughter fills me up when a hard little girl joins our table and gets busy chewing one big chicken leg after another and swallowing one big morsel of naan after another. My teeth are on the boil when I ask a little fellow, hanging about with a mobile game, if the hard little girl can also eat an elephant and he answers *how can that be, they are so big.* And in this way dividing my time between hilarity and the children, we are there. Moments away from our path. But first we have to receive our return gifts, thank the hosts, get invited by Aunt Doug to her place in the evening, shake hands and then hug and kiss our way out. We drop Diaz at Decawave and a million seconds pass in which he keeps looking back and Kaia with a motion of her hand sends waves of light and love and silvering laugh after him as into the sunset blush of shadows he keeps vanishing and when we catch the point she is making that she loves this boy so much, Deb pursues one eye with the other somewhere inside her head. My throat progresses seriously from the fringes of a growing thirst and Deb finds in the gift hamper juice packs and the horizon begins to run ink and my eyes close and Deb makes a loving gesture and sound and it always works and I have become what I am because of all this love. I tell her to give me some of her music loudly and she does and with these strengths I become strong and drive them to the society gate and then take the shortcut to school to attend grade XII farewell and then shortcut the whole function and get out while the gates still exist. Relations are a sum of doorsteps and I go straight to the bedroom and announce let's go to the Dougs and Kaia says *Chitra just called and they are waiting* so she calls them and Sandy says *come come* and they are people who are just a mile long from our house so we go and everyone's in their pyjamas lounging on a big mattress on the floor and they look revived from a sitting sleep of sorts and we have to remove our shoes and without my heels I feel so underwritten and hunger is a fixed want but when dinner is announced, I say, *I am not hungry*, however, persistence and insistence rescue me from the sofa to the dining table and then later on the sofa I shove Kaia around in my jokes but it's only noise. In the meanwhile, Diaz arrives looking for home here and the funniest things need not happen at the end because boy is he hungry and facilitates the emptying of dishes faster and talk circulates again and the largely younger audience is in a tingle with stories of Constantia and then the great Uncle whose eyes by night sink into the other world takes over from me and he opens his squeaky stories at the end of which he invites us to celebrate his 90th birthday and Aunt Doug tells Deb and Diaz you owe a gala celebration to your parents on their 25th and we all go down and stand like border people outside the gate. Night is half done by the time we are home. I hold Kaia's face in my sleep and in a dream my whole body executes a jerk and the hand with it and she wakes up yelling *pagal ho gaye ho kya* and I say *what is it? What happened?* and she says *you slapped me* and I realize that I did and explain that I saw a dream in which my whole body jerked and the hand with it too and she starts her ridiculous piercing laugh and Deb hears it and next day we tell her about it and she says *oh that's why you were laughing* and I fear we give away too much information in the night hours.

One parking has been given to Khan. Alto is outside, covered in the dust of misinterpretation which it sheds as I drive to the metro station. I am in my live-in clothes, a home man, standing, waiting outside the transitioning building; an imposing structure but this is just one. By long habit I know we don't remain the same whether inside, outside or passing through a place. Today I face the consequences of being me, reaching a marginal position with the extraordinary I experienced in Hategarh. Now it is just a disconnected picture of people, places and events. Kaia is hungry and snatches the kinnow from my hand I have brought for her. She laughs seeing that I saw that. The beyond song I don't hear anymore. Diaz notes that I am quiet and keeps gazing at me to see what is wrong with me, pats my head and keeps asking and they all say *he is going back to being himself again* and Diaz says *like he went to Australia, he was new only for a short while* but I explain next day in the morning as Deb, Kaia and I get into the lift at 7.30 that I needed Sam to bring me to this point and his function in my life was just that and Kaia smiles to herself.

Mull over the only world I know as real or may be this life is a copy. The moon is also a trite bigger in the window over me. I need additional time but Kaia doesn't even allow me that. She shuts the transformative alarm and creativity shifts to next day. A door may open for the maid but another may not for me.

4.

Precognition

The weather is getting into a corner but winter is still a giant. At 3.15 am, what I am doing, is what I am fit for. Looking vainly for a mystical release by plucking methi, palak and soya. At 4.30, I switch on my small laptop lamp, an apocryphal candle in the window against the present mists of the season. It illuminates my face, some silver in my hair but mainly it exposes my truth in ruins. Here I try to make meaning of the earth. Here I try to write the waiting story. Here I delve in infinite patterns called literature otherwise also called art and music at other times. Here I, a dead man, practice embarking immortality. Then in the small pleasures of the dawning light, colours slowly appear and with them my son and he introduces his veins to me in a rough cutting hug across my face. In that hug, he tries to grasp what I am but what I am, comes out when I am alone. For example, in the evening, when shadows grasp each other in foreplay, I leave for the metro station. I am not a cultural being. I only seem to possess the world as a civilised human being but I am a serpent in the story. I have the power to make my victim immobile. I am a dragon. Fire-breathing words when angry. A monster in an erotic female universe, chained and locked up in some supernatural chamber where I possess centuries, spawning fictional female fantasies in adventures of seduction. Whereas, the woman I am walking towards belongs to a spiritual order and as I fight my eyes from staring at fantastical females, I pretend that I have new eyes only for her. Kaia will always have this virgin character about her as she smiles at me, walking down the ramp. With great concern, she watches me, going to the traffic side to put her bag in the back seat and says *someday a car will hit you.* It would be the right thing I feel. She gives me the day's full report and when we reach home, I hand her over to Deb. I expect some new horror but end up watching *Signs* once again. Kaia is compared to Bo, sitting in Deb's lap. I also take turns to grab her. Deb thinks her bum is bony. I say *let me feel it.* When she gets up I feel it and say *it is not* and she exclaims *my bum and bony*! I have to lose some weight. Diaz comes. He kisses everyone and hugs me with a folklorish century of strength.

The morning is a crowd of sunlight and rain and rainbow and heat and cold and wind and calm and fall and spring and butterflies and robins. By evening, I begin to imagine Russian newsreaders with wings made of myths. And then comes Kaia. The female decorum of her garments is under great stress and a day of food does not pass when I am not fed by the sight of her. She saves me from doom. To celebrate my 25 years with her, I want to have a different event, a tour of magic perhaps. It's only now that I have learnt to have a hands-first approach to milk this marriage.

We reek of happiness at breakfast and play the part of comic characters. Diaz and Deb and I are humour hosting Kaia. After dropping her, I go to the driving test intersection. The test does not play any role in my inspiration but the fact that Diaz and Deb keep waiting for me for breakfast is. The evening is a touch of Kaia's silk on my skin but she pulls it and says *Bug Bug I have been transferred* and from my store of negative experiences, I give her a positivity lecture but I can see some of the sky is lost in the depths of the sunset. Diaz is an early midnighter. As soon as he comes, he lifts up Kaia. He needs a DC costume now. She hides her face because he bites her cheek and carries her around but saying to me *papa papa I missed you.* Kaia says *should I speak to someone about my transfer?* I tell her *you see to that but after two years they will bring you back.* She says *yes that is better.*

The beyond forces are roused at this hour. *I sense strong fire when I write about you, Kaia, my armful wife. I am so happy that I longed upon this country of love that you were and are and will be, where your maidens met in the narrow straits once. I have no regrets as your widely female places make me a debauch. There are women who emanate so much feminineness but my religion is you, my only female, where the sun lies in each kiss where each kiss is called by a name in a book I am still to write. My culture is a kiss-culture on the sunburnt suns. And love is resigned to an adult time when I am with you, seducing insanity. You intoxicate me. You have this amazing quality of staying well within the boundaries of feminine womanhood unlike others who age and change. There are some people who are on one side of blessings but you are on both sides of them. Whatever that means! O Kaia, Kaia, in 25 years, you have come to absolutely control me because in my blood passages, you have sown seeds of passion with what were originally lips.* This is my love legend which needs to see light of day but the dragons of ink put the day out of its own everyday very soon and now Deb has got a monologue going around my ears. Her breath is all fiery. The gaze is animal. Justin Bieber is on a musical road to Mumbai in May but I am at the front of God's war on all kind of idol worship and so an ecclesiastical debate ensues from our end but she does not brook any religious rhetoric over this. When we say *no*, we could be talking to ourselves. Her love becomes the stuff of embraces and kisses and Kaia and I capitulate. Diaz also nods to coming along.

Kaia speaks in a stuffed voice because I have said *no* to help her carry home all the stuff from her old office. This happens when I am on the point of possessing her; so now I can bid goodbye to the weekend's long night I have been looking forward to. Deb tries to play the arbiter. Both of them are now in the bedroom while I am beating words into my book in the study. A climate of increasing heat and unlimited thoughts become the gaps. I get the answer. I say *I will come* but now she says *no need*. Sometimes her eye has an old dominance like the eye of death's empress.

The aesthetically aging Mr. Sitaram picks up Kaia at 900 for TKD. He will give her enough confidence until her bones are set to drive on alternate days to their office. Booked Deb's tickets for her fantasy pilgrimage to Justin Bieber's show. She has come out of the caterpillar years so well. How thoughtful she has become, how sensitive, how loving, how empathetic, how understanding. She will shortly write a card message to her mother that will make her cry. Tonight's popcorn poster says *Good Fellas*. I like the expression *'don't bust my balls'*. Birthday exploitation begins from today.

It is midnight and Kaia's face is a roomful of people drifting towards tears and other services of the mood as she reads Deb's card but Diaz erases their effect with his 51 kisses in a 51 kiss-embrace. At breakfast, the mock managers are at work, laughing at each of her gestures, words, facial expressions until she asks *am I a clown?* Mock management is very important. It is a guard against erosion of intelligence.

We are at Ambience mall. With naked heat I watch the women. How they borrow ideas from moonlights, sunsets, sunrises, noon, afternoon etc. Some wear the woman so well. Some wear the female so well. Some go through elaborate clothing rituals with a century of clothing to look good. Some show taxidermic perfection with very little. Kaia looks pretty and young and colourful: blue high-neck, black jeans, pink lipstick and her complexion. She certainly wears both the woman and the female very well. Diaz walks behind me, light surrounded and almost strangled by his own hair. He has been through several hair methods but after the haircut, he says *now we look like each other* but I don't think sons are their father's soul successors. At the restaurant, the welcoming woman gives us a sensual smile from end to end. Buddha, the waiter, attends to our chaos with impeccable service. Sound of any kind does not invade his smile. A lot of food and some jokes and laughter and ice cream later we cross the Babel bridge to midnight and the home-road in my head lights up. Tomorrow's is a peripheral light passing us by at the end of each moment's spectrum, so we make this ink meeting of wishes and presents and cards intense. Then when the blue begins to move into its place in space, I map her body and the morning is all air and light.

The theme is birthday in spring. My mythological offspring decide and plan the day and outing so we are in Cyber Hub. It is a metaphor-and-simile-coated small safe world. A place of graphic inspirations within this dust and debris wrapped city. Here the knowledge of the real world is set aside by the food, the music, the drinks and the women in multiples of skin wrapped in snake clothes. I imagine meeting them at the outposts of mating. We level our years and other differences with love, affection, jokes, laughter, teasing etc. Kaia has to check me as I say *sex session* and then Diaz says *she said suck session* whereas Deb had said *succession*. Diaz slams me in the car with his music that can impact anyone of my age with insomnia but the trip was already deteriorating as soon as we entered the restaurant. We all have been slain by Taco Bell's food but it is Diaz who gets diarrhoea.

God recalls the sky. He will be in solitude today as Church has been cancelled due to Undo bhai visiting us with his nephew and family. He still gets a long unknown look in his eyes sometimes. His evolution hangs on the side as long as he is with them and they all need intense nirvana from him as soon as possible. The solution lies in the hands of the one whose birthday we are celebrating through three back to back days. Three days in which time becomes fluid, flowing this way and that way and not coming to an end. When the shape of rays changes, the guests leave. I say *let us celebrate sleep* and forthwith sleep like an artist of sound slumber.

Kaia's head temperature is high. She must have got only a yard of sleep as she worked on her files late night. Long day at school, then I follow my mouth home, then make sleep in bed until on the telepaths of psionic sleep, I pass by my wife's face and in its wake is her beautiful storm body that connects with my dust and it rises on its feet because it is 7.45 pm. She is a champion of inside noises and I hear her finishing sentence *how can you sleep when I am working and commuting.* We watch the Oscars and, oh boy, the old maidens are flavoured with makeup and the young have fictional bodies in skin multiples (as somewhere else) but over here, fitted out in gold and silver. In bed, Kaia's face is warm against mine and the rest of her is summer rushing about and through me. I sojourn a little longer in the dissipating moistures and wonder if there is a ceremony road of celebrations for us to mark our silver anniversary this year.

Sleep-walk this morning, sleep-read psalms but after one and a half cups of tea, I am afloat on waking wings. I am always walking around with a solution in my head so in the evening I cut the umbilical cord of sleep with an alarm so that Kaia does not find a snoring house caused by me even though I must tell her that we are created in our sleep, we destroy ourselves when awake. I do not want to be controlled by sleep. I do not want to be controlled by food. I do not want to be controlled by the physical whether it lies under or on or around the skin. I can't help it.

Come back to a locked house but the sabzee kadhai is open, the roti lid is half closed, the akhni pot is open, Diaz's pyjama, underwear and a few others are flung across bed and the balcony. Surely, there is a back theme to this. He didn't stop for the afternoon to catch up. Anyway, pace only grows here and I have no predecessor in what I am going to do. Deb opens the door with her key and catches me sitting at the table with my fingers deep into the dish and my mouth filled with rice, dal, veg and roti and gives me a one-way smile that says *you will be valued as quite a cute souvenir.*

5.

Before the season's fires

*T*heatrical skies are in close vicinity and clouds keep the sunrise far. Finally, the latter gets mixed up with sunset. Pigeons evoke this mix-up all day long in the balconies. Try to skip meals throughout the day but slowly slip on the evening's gradient and eat some rice, veg and daal. Kaia has no idea that I am writing a book on her. She comes back happy and makes me sit near her on the bed saying *you are very sweet*. Develop body terms with her immediately; looking forward to a wine like night. I will distil her into my fired brain and live on its cooling memory for the rest of the week.

A sun-supplied morning today with tea in bed. I grip her in a zodiacal embrace, then word nodes from our nature develop into an argument and then flower into a fight and then she experiences the wand pull of the spell of litanies and happily I take her to church. After the service, she comes out with a zodiacal glow and runs into Undo bhai's estranged wife. The daughter is a silent bearer of moons, an ambassador of moonlight fairies, a kidnapped fish-woman imprisoned in reincarnation caves, aglow in the afterlife light of stars. Wilderness should be easy with her and I wouldn't blame the angels who chose to lose their original self. We all encompass the wife's raven monologue in which she is blaming poor Undo bhai for everything. Lunch is a divine event with kofta curry on the menu again and Diaz consumes it all in an existentialist's binge.

A conference of eyes this morning in a room of nonsense. Kaia's face is blood set against Diaz's who refuses to fill exam forms for government jobs for which she is such a champion and wants to make him too. She ends the high pitch of screaming on me, referring to me in plural anonymity. *Dumb people! Nobody says anything!!* Sounds made in a rush, anyway, fade with the day and Kaia looks happy in her skin again and pours some of her happiness into mine. The sari fabric on her stretches to maturity. The rouge lands like sunset below the eyeliner and we set out in her alcoholic lights to meet Mr. Sitaram, a man of different silvering, his eyes circles of centuries, but he too looks to me like a wife survivor and I drive him and his wife and Kaia to the Air Force auditorium for their company's Annual Day.

Carnival of colours today that gives winter its last warning to get off the calendar. Today, the world folds up and explodes in colour and after half a day of dissolving new beauty into their worlds, women in half clothes, shadowed by fully painted winds, reign in the flying inks and the festival's subversion. My body feels all wrong without its weekly touch of my woman's. The weather has also not made its peace as yet. On top of that, Diaz announces with the freshness of a new bee's sting that his Convocation is on 9th May, one day prior to Bieber's concert. So we have another family conference going into several verbal rounds and it is decided that the return flights have to be rebooked, one for him a day prior to ours. Finally, my aging atoms experience molecular winnowing and I face sleep. A mitigating pigeon coos almost the whole night below a passing gold-growing moon. At 3.15 am, I wake up again sleep-faced.

Mr. Sharma, the carpenter, is a mushroom of meditation. I just find him growing on the sofa one day. The sun jumps on either side of him and his company for several days until the study, on which they are working, begins to drift into shape. Kaia has taken a vacation for this. Her arms have grown because only their faint ends are visible in the sawdust vortexes. On the final day, she is seeking perfection, erasing with the men, their dust, their faults and them from the finished study. She extinguishes herself with exhaustion and a severe backache.

A new sunrise over a distant sawdust mountain and in her love's shadow, Deb carries Kaia to Uma Sanjeevni for physiotherapy, where over a couple of days, she receives a new body, fit to carry out the work of the universe again while I involve the day and dusk in housing the books in their shelves. Kaia's cured smile is directed at me with her standard charm and some praise: *he loves books.* What a success she is. I don't even argue with failure. For so many days, it was difficult to find the sun in her face. But love's grass has grown long. Must feed on it. Her hard, angry shell falls off at night and the woman that she is, enters the bed. She sits holding my hand and prays and then the lights are off. I press her all over. To my vision, taste, nose, skin, ears and the sixth sense. I own each day and night I love her but sweating comes not as planned.

I watch her as she descends the steps of Boom plaza in the evening. *My! You have reached in half a century, a statistical attractiveness very few women can.* Multiple are the doors of pure delights of a mature woman and yet she has to gift-hop to another shop. We are invited to Dougs' house for a prayer meeting! Their pastor's stomach keeps grinding ingredients of holiness at regular intervals until the meeting reaches a sacred temperature when the preacher takes over. He is like a falcon of God and Sumer's mother-in-law watches him warily like a wide-eyed pigeon.

I am squeezing some light out of Kaia in the black hole where the lifts are. The doors open and in the subtitle of the lift lights, she steps in and her bags with her and she says *it is the best send-off today* and then leaves on my cheek a month of redness from her lipstick. A glowing shape on my subterranean skin. The whole day is a gap, until the evening when she enters the house with the effect of new space. Oh! She is so much. A binder and un-binder of the snake. She can even banish the apocalypse.

6.

Members of the same space

$\mathcal{T}$he street is full of rain monsters. Invading the day are moth phantoms from the night. Butterflies are adrift in the meadows. I have to purchase poems. Ink is not responding. The creator's face is missing from imagination. Marriage has fallen silent. I am making doodles of loneliness. All this because Kaia has left this morning for Ludhiana on a work tour. Diaz and Deb can only manage popcorn light and make me watch *The Accountant*. There is plenty of bed tonight in the plenty of empty night. Someone comes and puts off the plenty of empty light and switches on the AC.

Today waits to be written because you aren't here. Without you the air is not blowing in its lane. Without you same is not today. Good has been removed. The audience is not happy. I try to reignite life on the four burners. Which world is longer, I can't decide, yesterday's when you went, today's when you aren't here, or tomorrow's when you will return? Sleeping alone in bed is a kind of death by comparison. Marriage is not everyone's comedy. Tonight it has ceased to be mine. 3.15. I peer out. Stars have not been announced tonight.

It has been closing time for the neem tree all along. But today it does not cover the Mobilio's bonnet with dry leaves and twigs. Today it opens for work, all freshly green. That means Kaia is back. The thought fills me with the orgasmic rapture of dragons. Today in the afternoon, we will have lunch together and tonight, in bed, my arms will be complete.

It's a mile-strong walk from Spar parking to Evok but Kaia is unrelenting. She has to buy some furniture. After that we wait for Diaz, sitting on the ramp outside Pizza Hut. My eyes are tightly employed, watching episodes of the sunset, outlines of the season, night's storylines, women sparkling in clothes made from night's skin. Some bodies cast no shadows. The earth simply vanishes from below their feet. Suddenly the future begins to move faster. That means Diaz is approaching us and I look away from transgression and expand into higher humanity. In the lesser voltage of McDonald's, Kaia and my marriage of smiles comes to an end when self begins to play a part in it. Diaz rushes at us with accusations like *we don't go out anywhere.* I ignore the part which has *Shimla mirch on weekdays* but want to lash out when I hear *kofta curry on weekends.* My final emotions on the matter are to repeat the execrable kofta curry the very next day. The Mobilio is shadow-led in dragon silence. Deb tries her best to be half on either side, helping to remove our stares from each other's faces by controlling light and love. The falseness of fists dissolves as Kaia fills my tale as I fill her arms. I need more night and I lose the alarm for at least one more hour.

Life is not chapter based, moving from 1 to 10 but it goes back and forth. I have finished school magazine work and can pick up writing again. Yesterday, I cleaned up the study, so that books can get more involved with me and today I will give myself a more edited look.

It is Good Friday today and the guest preacher, a model of leadership and language, brings us the revelation of God and helps deliver us from the effects of our own presbyter's sermons. The cross is a very pretty object to hold especially with Jesus' statue on it. But more than that, it asserts the truth of our existence. As the community of the cross, we have a very difficult job to do: explain the way of the cross to the world. I will make an attempt. God made a breakthrough through Christ by making his love for humanity a historic event some two thousand years ago, changing everything from giving us a weekend to taking that love forward through forgiveness of sins. Good Friday's claim upon us is this that we have a choice: either stand there and mock the Son of God and go back to the world or receive this story of love, in faith and find the way to God's heart forever.

How Kaia wears the woman. I look at all her details which she loves and will invent more. As the sun presses into a sunrise, she rises into it like a wing. She has office on Saturday today for the first time.

A lily's touch this morning has. Easter bring us back to our own reverend. A sermon sums up the whole Bible like psalm 23. God does not give a sermon but he grants lips and a tongue to his speaker. Our reverend should earnestly pray for such gifts to be bestowed upon him. What is the difference between the temple and the church? The difference is the sermon. God never preached a sermon in the Old Testament but He preached a sermon in the New Testament.

Changing years to moments with her beauty is Kaia. Her beauty booms as she drags us once more to the furniture mall after church to buy a recliner and lights. I am into age now but I need another look at my years. *You have filled me, Kaia, an empty adult, in these last 25 years.*

As the sunset circles the house, we make intense moments of summer and between the horizons and on either side of the hemispheres and what is sky skin by day, the same is camouflaged in moonlight, galactic paradoxes, such as star ways, part eyes, part bioluminescence and speeding night and before you know, it is May by midnight.

7.

Spectrums of beyond

Sunrise is a custom but still a distant light when we embark on this journey by plane. A sun is found in Deb's window, out of which the horizon rises and then as it falls like an intense tide, flat screen Mumbai, the face of India, becomes visible. On reaching the hotel, the only activity is emotion as Kaia rejects the place outright and its disguised vicinities. We take our sour expressions out to Chaupati where the water is not very broad but Kaia and Deb take more than their share of the sand a little beyond the surfing edge of the water. We look for some sunny food but all we get is sun-nourished chuskis. Finally, we are able to establish a meal but by the time we are at Colaba, we are coping with Kaia's anger again. By now we have got used to agitated recreation and leaving her, the three of us march through and around the Gateway of India. We lose sight of her and Deb's childcare instincts take over. She goes in search of her and brings her to us where we are sitting and then Deb chaperones her as she expresses her desire to also see the monument. The spectrum of our combined states of mind match the colours of Colaba and all of a sudden I spot a bright red iconic guest house. Kaia is elevated as this is a Christian place. We are shown two rooms. In the dim light of a wide-open neighbouring dorm, sitting or standing or lying on bunks are a lot of girls, wearing only a narrative for an underwear or two. They are young fairies in peak form, climbing the mists on some north eastern mountain. I love getting involved with my writing sometimes. Later, like accidental customers we walk into Churchill, an old Parsi restaurant. The two ladies who own, run and serve the food are from the aging ranks of the old conquerors and undisputedly untouched by time. Their manners and cuisine deliver the soul from Mumbai's general hawker styles. Time spent here is total comfort. It has distinguished the day from its beginning and ending. We make a late return and use sleep to save our eyes from the soreness of Hotel Abyss and in no time we are hypnogogic swans, the greater and the lesser, across each other's beds. Way past midnight, I cross into a waking state and am playing eyes with the night and step out into a faint lane outside the room with my camera but it is not able to develop the focus. The triangle of senses however, can make out the circumstances that are built in and around this place and they are the very make of hell, for example, a visual voice that I am either seeing or hearing.

Before I can misinterpret the illusion, it is morning and Kaia and I make sensory contact with flesh and blood staff. She makes the payment but I know there is no need to try to even introduce brain to these people. She is at the spur of a delirium trying to do that. We check out and check into Holy Cross guest house. We have breakfast in a South Indian joint where the waiter has the voice of a banana, soaked in yogurt and the owner is a sambar prototype with lentil flour paste smeared across his forehead and in papadum crisp lungi and shirt. His one eye, as big as an idli, is on everyone and everything. The other is dipped in the rasam of his brain. He is pretending to toy with his midday pan. A whole row stands at attention on a plate. He lights his lighter's gas with a matchstick. Other customers watch us as we incapacitate ourselves with several courses while there is a fresh rise and fall of feet around us several times. His smile, when we leave, is nothing short of a sweet dish sequel. The aftermath of this meal and all the walking we did yesterday is that I find it hard to walk. I need some sort of medical means to do that. A clinic close by is on offer. It is inhabited by a retired medical being, his degrees extending to sigma, and who himself seems to be on a lost medical voyage in a dying ship. I offer him my story. He makes some notes, part of which he puts on a medical certificate for me. We have to break the narrative to buy medicines etc. and then I am dragged off to various beaches. The most notable one is Marine Drive, a long slim favour to the city of intricacies, stretching like spent time that can be spent again for want of anything else. Want to go down and sit where the others are, their legs growing into the sea. We rate the sunset as one of the finest and photograph its twilight version even when it is submerged where the crabs see it better for a little longer. The famous Mumbai street dinner is part food, part magic. We eat until we are outside digestion jurisdiction and besides, our eyes are so night-like and the deserted roads on a death course that we decide to leave. We sleep in one room, locking the other one up. In about a third part of the light from some dim bulb, I wander into the corridor and get an intense feeling that human existence here reached a saturation point years or decades ago and now there are those who cannot cross the borders from the spirit world, asking to be saved by an embrace. Something here is frightened of blessings too. Night is a time when this invasive feeling grows very strong.

The trip is college-crossed. Diaz follows the goodbye kisses and hugs from us into the airport. He has to reach Delhi today to attend his convocation where he will receive his scholarship money and citation for his wonderful performance. We are back and Deb goes to sleep but our mouths are in position for some breakfast in the dining room. I find my allegiance to sleep too. When I wake up, afternoon light is sawing through the room and Kaia's silence, as she tidies up the place, is sawing through me and I know immediately what is to be done and wake up Deb. We dress and use English as travel language since the journey incorporates a ferry with foreigners and a train with foreigners. From the coast, a narrow-as-a-palm-line path moves up and up and it is so long and hard that even a smile becomes a task. Then it all opens out like a hand and we are in front of the first Elephanta Cave . I am already better on knowledge about the place from Deb's mobile research. Inside a hewn rock cut cave, there are idols with future finish personalities that, archaeologists believe, could not have been possibly made by humans. We are little people in front of their mountain bodies and fortress faces. You become a different person and stare transfixed at the entities without a 'can leave or can't leave' option but I am sure, and Deb agrees, that this place catches the night like no other place on the face of the earth. I purchase a few souvenirs of some places that are the forevers of the earth and find a place on the descent to eat and then catch the last train out of the dying edges of the iron green mangroves before it all shuts down by 6.00 pm. I take the support of water to shoot a video of the sinking twilight and against it, the Gateway and the Taj Palace also beginning to doze off.

Kaia and I participate in the sunrise. Keeping pace with the morning is not at all difficult as we slowly sip lovely tea at the dhaba and then opposite it have the loveliest idlis, the tastiest sambar, the juiciest bondaloos, the hottest chatni and of course the most involved chai. They may not be in a state or national or international book of breakfasts but the dawn of customers they get, is ample proof of how good they are. At the hotel, we wipe the stain of sleep from Deborah's eye by telling her a great lie which we ourselves didn't know at the time that it was a lie. She bubbles around happily and happily we head to Air India office only to be told by a very sweet lady, who also feels sorry for Deb, that the price is 11,000 per person if we postpone the flight by a day to attend the concert. No way. God's way. Colour appears in Deb's face by and by with the realisation that we tried very hard which she later shows by her overwhelming behaviour, more familiar to the eye and the ear. Afternoon is strongly carved into her face and demeanour after shopping at Crawford Market and exotic dining at Pa Pa Ya. We make a search for culture in the souvenir shops. At quarter to six we leave for the airport. In the confined space of the economy class, I try to comprehend various spaces. It will come in handy after the next month when we will be six in a two and a half bedroom flat. The journey precipitates towards its end but until it does, future has to wait for its turn. I will cosy up with it too.

Undo bhai is at church. He is sowing shadows somewhere but Kaia will try to get him into an old age home. I am reconciled to my shape but Diaz begins *mission slimming dad*. He has a doing heart but tonight he is in some other orbit. Kaia worries about his profile pic with his girlfriend Nile. Deb takes a lot of interest in my diaries, written long ago. She has such a dreaming heart but she is also becoming a thinking and feeling woman and yet so much growing is assigned to each of us from 8 to 18 to 80.

8.
Invading minorities

I need to drink her from her flowery-flaring, pink petalled nighty. Kaia looks sexiest in hurry-wear. I look age-set, whatever I wear. She is aroused like a mountain and we fold up into a peak.

We all need night and sleep but my time with both is up at 3.15 at which time I cook for an hour while partaking tea and daily spiritual particles from the audio Bible, then in the buried light of my small laptop lamp, I work towards a sunrise. The sun rises, knowledge returned. Reasonable end of office for Diaz at Decawave. This was Kaia's happy hope. Happy hope meets Undo bhai at church and it is lost. We have lunch at *Imperfecto* and then Kaia wants him dropped to his old age home. I say *no* and immediately her face is in a fit of fury. An inferno in her eyes. And her words come out of an abyss. *This is my car! And he is my brother!!* Diaz is like a weapon on my side but he speaks in a soothing butterfly voice to me *it's all right* and puts the wasps and scorpions inside me to sleep and I drop Undo bhai at his old age home. Part of a marriage is to pretend. So we have a little day left to pretend everything is all right until I am ready to drive again into a buff sunset at Raheja's to waste time and money on *Wonder Woman.*

A personal sun rises over Kaia and me. Its special effects will haunt thousands of suns every day until it is repeated because I get a happy personal tour while escorting her on her official tour to Jaipur. Sun happy, Shatabdi progresses with our morning. A back theme to this morning is: this world of sensations should have happened in 1992 but then again this is time's way to be perfect. If clichéd is to be romantic or vice versa, twenty five years later then, that's the way to be perfect too. This distance from then till now must play its part and bring this partnership ever closer. The sparkle matters even now. But you know what? There's always potential for the weird. My waking dream without a break takes me from the platform into a waiting vehicle and then a five star ITC hotel and now she must hold my eye because food is my woman but sweet women at the reception have my eye too. Yes, I have the eye and they have the look that still seems like women's but have bodies like saw that can cut through any man's. What adds to the chaos is the rich fragrance where the musk of home must get in the way but after Kaia is gone on her tour, I am cocooned by time. Try ink but it fails me and it seems I am sold to waiting till she returns and then we go and eat out and return and my eye becomes her only dress and then time becomes what it is: chaos. And the body need not feel young for an orgasm. I am overrun with it as my 52 year old naked skin tries to distinguish her 51 year old naked skin from the smooth white fresh satin sheets. It feels like old honeymoon, the one we never had twenty-five years ago. What a timing! Twenty-five years ago we were on a poker-face date at Maidens.

After breakfast, Kaia makes her report and leaves for Kishangarh. I try writing again but again cannot get even an inch of the cursor to move on the laptop. Check out at 2.00 pm and go out into the dead summer heat of the city and get the feel of the place. I am good at that. Leave me somewhere and I will tell you what consumes the place. Oh my!! I am completely impressed with womankind's phenomenon. A school of stars will attend the living nights of deep forests if Kaia is there. Her native mouth is talented in the ways of being kissed. Her china is so smooth like viable vessels of heaven. And I, a beast of the earth, cast in daily ebony, am so very much contrasted when I hold her and lie against her. She is the lifespan of a man's happiness. Beauty's traditions forgive me for such a long lifespan of love-making. And yet hoping and thinking of how true is her poetry, cut out by the passionate knowledge she has of herself and of the man who wants her all the time. The common people forget the moments that awe them but not me. I remember when I meet life. I ask no questions. Only I feel and sense her presence. We get off at Gurgaon railway station. Deb tries to book a taxi but sector 1 cannot be located on the GPS. Was this real? Anyway, we take an auto and come through the detritus map of the old quarter, looking like a pair of dust-devils ourselves. Try my best to map the human landscape that lies outside this tinsel township in these two days with my camera. Woman is the tunnel into future and marriage is schooling. When I am dead, I will be happy that it was life that got me.

I am a middle entrepreneur, that is, I keep working on expanding my middle in spite of Diaz's capsules. It's a folly to be in bed with Kaia. A desert storm from her nostrils keeps lashing against my sleep door and dream windows because Diaz has gone to a late night party. And when he comes, her body launches out like a grenade to blast him but he slams head on into it his dragon grin, blowing out a little cloud of skin from her face.

Ink from the quill of the sun this morning, writing subtitles from previous night on our page. *You can't open your mouth* Kaia says. *Yesterday when I was speaking to him you didn't say a word.* There is an imaginative gap after my statement *I will not sing your tune.* The skies make a beginning again and light comes back to us as our good friend and we all go out because money wants to fly out of her purse. The destination of Rs. 14,000 is FOCUS Academy of Competitions for Diaz's admission. I need real legs made of steel or something. Kaia stops to look at the clothes landscape at sector 14 market. I show symptoms of great fun watching *Breaking Bad*. Smiles, excitement and traumatic shock do not reach an end.

There is never less to love. Jonah and Dona, a generation darkened by tragedy, arrive. She is skin-thin but within, she can endure a lot of things including a silent storm of feelings. Jonah has only sunsets and without boundaries. He is also used to a love vacuum, though he can very quickly transcend to love, life, light and laughter. Watching last episode of *Breaking Bad* today. Have felt so connected to Walter White for so long. Face insomnia till 2 am as an after effect. Fall asleep when the ocean advertises itself by dropping a big piece of rain on us and dousing summer's blazing guns.

The only human in this paragraph is Aunt Doug whom we visit briefly with our masks of love since she has had her city eyes operated. She lies in bed with immortal weariness and yet looks like a major benign theme. The eye under the patch blinks as its memories of light get restored. Sumer's wife, Divyani, the hostess of subtle humour, enters and serves us sweets but there is a war of wings going on in the dim light of loose ends. Diaz refuses to take the tray from me to pass around and she comments *I can see what you will do in a board meeting* which has to be understood in the light of her smile and wakes up my Rowling creatures and they claw and peel my mood off. There is already a mythical one in my sinus. A wingless one is wrapped around my feet. Millions of distances later, we are in an MGF mall and I am in a three-headed mood. The KFC fellows are slow like eggs in a geomythical swamp so in a voice that is the counterpart of thunder and with a breath that is the ancestor of fire, I hurl some virgin abuse at them but Jonah wags his saint's tail and says *you only called them bloody fools, idiots and bastards.* They are so amphibiously clumsy and slow that now Kaia is in the grip of the oriental spirit to shout, scream and hurl insults and like a double-headed mother of Godzilla, she gets up and stomps off to the counter to tell them to hurry up with the food but once the oily fried chicken arrives, gravity propels us to settle down, the fire-breathing drops down to rats' breath and a wave of flashing teeth later, awash with ice-creams, we return to being single-headed.

Shovelling through early morning with temptations. We are at the Tehsildar's office for some work. She has a long pull on me as I watch her run about. Post-midnight, the kids have pancakes and games while I finish transcending days of dry wife days. Flesh feels so fortunate to be flesh. Later, she gets out of bed and the grown-up kids receive an eye that becomes the theme for the rest of their night. Some being she is, other than being Kaia.

Jonah is depressed, sitting in the open window, legs dangling out, staring at the city's horizon. I write a post about my feelings on FB: *Perceptions of the end. The other day, I watched you sitting in the window all by yourself, looking out at what could have been and what if it had been possible to get going, without a worry, in this world, just like everyone else. You see every day, the morning growing from start and ending in darkness like a recording that plays over and over again. You feel the wind, hear the birds chirping, see the children laughing and playing but you know, the orchestra doesn't support the song anymore. The song of love, you ask, where is it? In its place, there's left only the love to long for those who aren't coming back. You wish to become the music you keep humming but it doesn't help. You wish to become the portraits you keep looking at but it doesn't help. You can heap years and years on their memories but it doesn't help. The fast winds that took them away, do not count how many trees they uprooted. Sometimes you reflect on your growing up and you find that even the parameters of your childhood were never about chocolate and candies and toys and other things other children get by. But let me tell you that I wish you to keep moving because in keeping it moving, a fixed day's work of death becomes nothing. And the second thing is love. If there is and was any, love always wins out at the end.*

He doesn't even know about it.

With her hereditary facial powers, Deb shows us that she is in a parchment thin mood. She thinks that we are in a conspiracy against her passport process. She sleeps, keeping the whole day from sunrise to sunset as far from her as afterlife. At night, Dona, the bearer of apology on behalf of us all, exhibits a pre-existing divine ability and coos like a cosmic pigeon to win her over to us. *Oh Dona, you are a fresh myth that nobody else can become; small is the contest when you step in. You are the book of the day that needs a reader's love. You are the truth that even children are not resources of. You are the climate fish dream of. Egyptians would have to travel to future to collect that look and the world just caused itself to be better by bringing you in. Forgotten myths look for nobody else but you. Future comes back bored to you and goes back defiant as a fresh dream. Artists are not taught innovation, they still have to work on that look you give us and everyone else. You are a sticker of small truths on highways of books. Fish can be louder than you. Cultures find makeup boring when they learn about your simplicity. If I ever need a book sold I will write about you. You are nobody's replica, a singular standard of cultural sites of love that are dreamt.*

A measure of dawn. The sun is a widening disk over the plane of Gurgaon buildings. Windows are included in the following view: Clouds with legends. Raindrops like air pearls. Each drop with an address in this raindrop city. Community weather in the afternoon. People in rain portraits. Adult urban droplets. Moist parts in poses. This is the way I used to know summer before. Then a membranous sunset. The Equator's liquids rise again. Deb, Jonah and Dona go to the terrace. This is the rain for the young. The upper fluids curve in the heavens and fall with a dooming velocity. The tower is in a frenzy of a thunderstorm. The warped girls dance and scream in splashes of innocence. Then gradually development of only roof noise and then complete sonic silence. Jonah's ability to hear or to see is very acute. The geometry of the rooftops has admitted him a view, through the limits of the summer solstice night and rain, of the shape of a human at the far edge. The face lines are distinguishable from any breaks in the teeming darkness. Then whatever was prior to roof happens. The three of them make a parabolic descent in Nano seconds to the twelfth floor.

I didn't know Jonah has choir skills. Whatever it is, the singing has been accumulating. Diaz takes him to his fitness centre. When thy return, Jonah is performing acrobatics on the scooter and singing at the top of his voice, totally oblivious to the fact that centuries of crowds have been staring at him all along the road. I don't want to be his audience so I tell him to stop it but oh Jonah! *You have built years in one day. You are a song, Jonah, created from the first songs of angels. Creativity was spent on you and the future was finished in the past when you were made. Back in the mushroom days, when you parted from your first family, your second family had to compete for you with the hunters of songs. It was the dream-making Providence that saw your visions and saved you and which will transform the end accordingly because you are the battle that grows in its head. You are the emotional risk every story has to take because you are an alone rainfall, an unshared imagined rainfall. You are the Avant-garde of faith, a conservative of righteousness (which has cost you. Fortunes have this shocking habit). You are the first favourite of everything sinister but it's all a bubble in the end, a wonder of spent childhood and teenage. So don't worry because success finished building you long time ago and future respects you. You are the first freedom of a New Year's morning. You are a part of a thousand resonations that bring ends to meet from head to toe, oh Jonah! And it is good to share the ways of a rainfall.*

A dose of too many raindrops extinguishes Jonah's state of well-being. Kaia is playing a higher part in Dona's admission in some vocational institute. She looks faintly divine talking to people on her mobile seeking advice on my and her behalf. Jonah helps with the wind and the sunset by sharing with us episodes of his disturbed beginnings but he can move friendly twilight into position with his eyes alone. We are afraid that speeding night will bring uninterrupted apparitions walking on the long legs of shadows from that house in Hategarh where earth sometimes moves backwards in the faint lanes of hallucination. From the periphery of this supernatural contagion, I notice my son hasn't returned. He is certainly not a member of Early Return from his girlfriend's birthday party. Kaia is at the spur of a delirium.

9.

Each day is like a cocoon

She has gone to office but we have a full love house followed by a laughter drive around the city. We go around casting our day in great fun in malls and eating joints. I am surrounded by numbing fun. We even utilise tears. Even Dona shows great fitness for it. Jonah has to leave for Hategarh tonight. Everyone wants him to slip into a job. Tomorrow he has to join work in a mission school there. Diaz is selected by an American company.

Jonah has understood the pay but not the work. Rats, with ghetto blood in their veins and with looks, discussed elsewhere in this book, give him a kind of insidious smile as they shove him into unskilled rut for the day, like sitting at the gate on day one and dusting the furniture on day two and then on day three he goes through unspeakable struggle as he is asked to wait at a table where principals would dine at a meeting. His mother would have been there eating at the table had she been alive. And his grandmother when she was the head. He descends into jeopardised solitude and is seriously considering becoming luggage for the coffin bearers. In fact, he vanishes for some time but I cannot imagine him with his voluminous sunset hair, looking for a room in the graveyard, next to his parents' graves. Deb has received his text message in tribulation vocabulary and wakes me up and says *is there any more room in your silence? Get up and do something.* I need not tell her that this is not a storm of crosses. I text Jonah *we only attempt life. Please erase the dust of the place from your shoes and whenever you want, take the first bus out of Hategarh.*

Diaz's first day at his company, set deep in the direction of a growing sunrise. My exhaustion is revived by the time school is over. The body is undisputedly supreme. I am lifeless. My feet ache. But I can only be saved by getting debauched. There is a cry over my middle-age curves. Diaz is trying to deliver my shapeless body with green tea but catches me drinking Limca. I try to run it past him with a smile but he has declared a silent war of visual rage and doesn't come to the table to have chowmein which I have been able to make after the energy therapy. Can I allow him to happily dominate over me? Can I ever get used to the adult rule of my children over me?

I am the true admirer of Kaia's parts, every one of which has a new vocabulary and how they all speak to me, every time they get a chance. I am not somebody who knows love but I surely burn in love's intensity. Mine is not a slave's marriage. I am among the dreamers. There has to be poetry in our thoughts; poetry in our creativity. I'm new with thought but I have to tackle a lot of old life in me. Tonight is tortured by delight but before that we watch *Silence*.

The world is all set to happen for Dona. All thanks to Kaia. She is served success with her admission in a YWCA professional programme. Kaia and I are past heavens and I am listening to the emptiness that follows it. The stars are ending but the racket the four young adults are making in the adjacent room is still the same. I am trying to touch in my mind this time tomorrow. We will be returning by owl moon from watching Spiderman at Raheja's.

My ankle and my knees need a hospital. I walk around like a broken husk with planter's fasciitis. Kaia comes early and she is right off at it and we visit the only budgetary hospital in the city. At home she prepares the hot and cold juices of healing for my feet. In hers just the salt moves but I am in debt to Deb for running a week of cold-and-hot-feet therapy. The swelling hell of the heel just needs her divine touch. Diaz gives the whole exercise a sweaty finish by boiling eggs for me and feeding me with his hand. Kaia talks about her crushing office work but we don't get it.

With my dieting, comes their popcorn and squash. My dietitian brings smoked chicken for me and mixes it with boiled eggs and serves me. The three of them are in the kitchen where instincts take over in popcorn fashion and the three of them are coming to a boil. A couple of hearts away from them are Dona and me, TV neighbours on a sofa. A little chaos later, I am trying to disengage them but our bodies get all mixed up. Chicken muscles in a tangled knit with hard boiled biceps. Deb screams at me *why don't you say anything to him?* Kaia answers her *he is afraid.* My mouth hangs. I might lose my gender over this but I decide not taking the bait and say *I won't fall into your trap.* You can lose your mind or find meaning. I decide the latter. Kaia chooses the former and shuts herself in the bedroom. This is a house of love, life, light and laughter for God's sake! Deb's love's outreach is longest but tonight even hers falls short of reaching me with the hot and cold water therapy and an episode of *Stranger Things*. Diaz makes me tense with his love. Now he has ordered a protein drink for me! But I must embrace this for his sake which means drinking a glassful of the horrible stuff every day! Weather in its wisdom: windy, stormy and cloudy. A rage tears up the sky. Humble rain abstains because humility is in falling. Horizon proceeds. Next day is founded and Dona's birthday begins. A day of light and life and laughter for the one who loves.

Each day is like a cocoon or a great snail inside its shell. Jonah has arrived though his path has many miles to cover and transforming the miles, on an expedition to celebrate Dona's birthday with us is Dididi with Simeon, Sana and the little girl. I hear a rushing of days when Jonah takes out his late mother's gold to transfer into my custody. I do it with a principled face but begin to feel like a partisan of ambiguity when Dididi refuses to even touch it. The day is debited with a celebration outside but first Kaia puts a hairstylist around Jonah's long tresses and very soon they are deposited on the salon's floor. He follows behind in the silence of the haircut, absolutely unhappy with the balance. Now at least the sun can get past it into what we can see is evidently a face. After two days of direction in which she also prays for my feet, Dididi and her train leave.

Life passes through me early morning. A lifetime of energies flow out of my two ends. It's like this is happening on a potential order from hell. Soon I am a series of pictures in a gallery of delirium either posing over the sink or pounding away on the commode. Truck faced, I endure the vomiting and the loose motions. I need to put some fresh breeze aside. I might as well have swallowed a shower of cactus. The nausea is unbelievable. I am not even the owner of my mouth. God is in His comfort cloud but I'll make Him a rainbow if this double shower stops. It is a risk to even fart so I must take leave today. Healing comes from lying on the good old bed but I keep the fly open. Diaz, my son of laughter, is not even the shadow of a smile these days. He comes and goes, comes and goes like a doodle of lightning.

Earth is a woman in the rain, blissfully outdoors, her clothes slammed against her body and I am a silhouette, wearing only the wind and want to throw off that too and not wait for her to be air-dry. For they who quit heaven, did so, when they saw the drenched lily, a ring of stars in her every smile, to take her from the day or the day from her. The blood of life is lustful passion. Must take to more praying in the morning. Due to breakdown of popcorn amongst us, not even half of us watch *Life*.

10
Kill death in literature

*K*aia's nighty is cut out of love prints from a tulip, azalea, begonia, foxglove, hibiscus, orchid and even a snap dragon. A flower wearing the wind. And I am on new sails, gravitating towards her in graphic passion. The blame is always floral. With arms unending, we hug and with lips unquenching we kiss but separate like forbidden lovers when I hear slippers scrape. After school, transition to afternoon. Time to establish relationship with two rotis and a kadaifull of rice, dal and sabzee and then break from my own reality to watch *The Walking Dead*, a show about a long night that is sometimes lost in a day. *At the metro station, dedicating my eyes to watch your way, it's the course of a song, with love and when I spot you I say to myself that one is mine. Your fire is easy. I can burn in it forever.* Diaz comes and kisses me. I say *go and kiss them* and he says *naaaah*. A couple of cosmetic hours in which *you softly mislead the night with your vanilla body, absorbing the moonlight through the window open behind me. Then my hustling heart wants to ride love and I bare your great adult bosom that needs a man's childlike grip and its childlike love.* Then an end of time sleep. Then again the draperies of the night close in on screaming space and time ends into a consciousness. Kaia's hand is in mine. I say *hallelujah*

and her hand jerks. 2.46 am. How am I able to see the clock? The tube light is on itself!!!

A little later at 3.30 am, I am still capturing night in my love book when Kaia takes the shape of day but with details of a sunset in her eyes and comes and stands near me in the study and tries to draw a conversation out of me. My hands forget their work and contribute to their kind of conversation. Breasts are the best guide to the rest of her. Moments of a lifetime, movement of laughter until she leaves for office. The breakfast also goes the smile way. For at worst, Dona is innocent. She doesn't even know the way her smile goes, says, she heard a breathing near her in bed at 1.00 am. That's the time I say *I felt something wrong in our room* and that is because when angels leave our side, darkness has a breakthrough. And then we get to that mind where we all feel and think the same thing and Jonah says *Uncle you need to keep a tight hold on Diaz* and Deb says *you should scold him* and I say *I cannot. I have achieved nirvana from the upbringing I have subjected you both to and the only thing I now want is that there should be no negativity in this house.* For this is a house of life, light, love and laughter. We are yet to reach our lowest, though. Ink gets into the gaps. The way I am, I don't know how I keep finding love. I am eating pears when Diaz comes back and boils and peels two eggs and serves me only the whites. I remind him of the eleventh commandment *thou shalt not throw the yolk away.* He says *there is a twelfth one thou shalt not consume cholesterol.* I give night a look or two and leave the online Bible on. It will achieve a breakthrough to good gloom while we sleep. I can't find any relative of comfort in bed since my partner's head is in my feet and I need my head and her head in the right place and I have to toss my brain about for some time and then bend the night over to reach down and correct her position.

Jonah and Dona are with me on a little shopping run and we leave the allowed tracks and journey into the past, to the frontier history of this place, to a time of polyphonic wilderness, and then to a wilderness past the lights, to a time when wilderness was a contagion like the pioneer instinct of humans who invaded and inhabited it.

A lot of ill-health has accumulated. We are Uma Sanjivni's peak patients, anyway. Dr. Lobhia examines us one by one in the order of illness: first Jonah's neck, then Kaia's wrist, then my heel and at the end Dona's nothing. The man radiates such control with his own questions and answers and only seldom advises health chemicals. I am in a general state of happiness which causes temporary anxiety but it's a walk through the praise park for Deb from Kaia for helping her and taking care of her. In Deb's book of praises by me, is also listed her participant level in opinions and arguments.

We have God for a lifetime so what if sometimes we miss meeting Him one day! I did that today. In the evening, against a fire sunset, Deb, Jonah, Dona and I watch *Dunkirk* at Raheja's. Diaz has office at his work place and Kaia has office work at home. She has another reason: the 'war at home' reason. Can't help but notice history's teeth bared at us in a grin of irony.

Dona's first day out to her college today. Throwing the early air around her is Deb. For Deb is the day. You can get a bit of your light from her like what the stars are still giving. But first she is strong. Dona is like a lily working its petals out in that strength. With her, Dona makes her first ever beginning, meeting her teachers, making friends and finding her way back home. Secondly, Deb is the essence of love. A woman or a man drying or dried of it can fill herself or himself up. Thirdly, Deb understands the acting creature. So when Kaia rings the bell in the evening, I sit up in bed and open the Third Reich. Deb understands the trick whereas her mother thinks I have been awake, reading. She is a royal picture, smiling down at me when Kaia exclaims *arrey, you are awake!*

Deb is an expert on the world. She knows what fragrance is. She is the first to have mathematical suspicions about things that are not mathematical. Like what Americans do. Or like paradoxes. Like the first smile, she rings hope and order and help and protection and liberty because when I refuse, she chaperones her mother to Ghaziabad, when down in the week, Uncle Fizzy fizzles out and has to be laid to rest next to aunts Holly and Little. She cannot be a mistake of atoms, being the first doodle figure in my life. She calls me up to get them out of the deformed watery gloom of the metro parking when they return because the Alto's battery drained out. She pops jujips into my mouth as I drive us out of there. She will be long in the tent, moving and making her years even though she keeps saying happily *the world is going to end, the world is going to end.*

I am dreaming morning. An early joy talk of birds draws me to the balcony and I catch the day with Nature there, both soaking in the music of the rain. A lot of life has been received here from this coupling. There is a first able twig on every plant. In most pots, there is time in snail state and at light's end, like little wagging fingers of

Nature, are the earthworms. Some greenery is hoping to climb up, reaching out in snake hands towards raptures of God. But it's the butterflies that receive the sky. They will be there awhile for after them comes the winter and that is when they become pathless. Grass is learning patience of light by crawling away from shadows. Weather's musicals are the vibes from a bee and a wasp. The sky offers some more rainforest later in the day. After dissolving some green into me, I am ready to bloom like a day because somewhere, in here, I encounter my essence. A creature's essence. It could be growing a sting. Or a thing's essence like becoming a colour. Whether you are down like the earthworms and the snails or up like the butterflies and the bees, you don't bring worthlessness. I go back inside but will be back for more colossal experiences.

The day is black now and a silent kind of talk is going on here at the dinner table. Diaz does not pass the main dish to Jonah. Dona and Jonah are anyway like depth lilies. Kaia has purchased another molehill. Deb tells me about it. I did not accompany her to the funeral so be ready to deal with a mountain now. I say *she didn't come to watch Dunkirk with us* and Deb says *that's so childish* and Kaia says *take revenge, take revenge*. Diaz picks up only my plate and Kaia smothers a smile. He and I watch *Leon the Professional*.

Must press the universe harder to get things to make sense. To resolve the unresolvable equations. Like why are simplified folk host to so many ambiguities, keeping us constantly polarised?

When lines of engagement open again, a comfortable debate over an ordinary issue of civilisation such as attending Uncle Fizzy's memorial service gets mired in the uncomfortable long matter of Jonah and Dona's stay here. We are certainly not simplifiers of the world. A civil moment is reached by afternoon and polarised peace made with Diaz opening a minimised conversation with his mother later and we leave for Dilshad Garden. Our energies merge. He navigates. I drive. He plays the songs. I listen with a sigh. In the little drawing room of Uncle Jean, we all sit face-surrounded and only traces of a stir can be made, if at all one wants to stretch an arm to take a song sheet or open the mouth to sing or turn the eyes in the direction of the sermon or the ear to catch the word bouquets building a picture of Uncle Fizzy. He was no brochure hero. In fact, he had always seemed to me to be on one extreme end of the fossil world. He never shopped for a face or a figure. In fact, he was like a breeze aside that does not move even a hair on your head unless provoked. I cannot say what percentage he was lion. A lamb in front of his late sisters, and what percentage an ace of his race but whichever was fiercer, was greater. But he kept the human side of him for the extreme end of each night when he went out and fed stray dogs and the extreme ends of the day when he went to the terrace and fed squirrels. Long was his way on the earth and a short one to some spirit world in sore need of his daredevilry. Sending him to heaven would be such a waste of the nightmares he can heap on the serpent people or the rat people or some such other menace people. But there is a reason for so much space devoted to him in my story. He is the second person I know who truly turned on the path of self-discovery. When he was younger, a rifle would have comforted him. A fishing rod would have occupied him for hours. He could pursue his enemies for days on end in self-defence. With vintage ability, he would have satisfied your craving for flesh with his cooking. His musical side could serve classical enchantments on a tabla. But in his later years, his heartbeat arrived like a lump in his throat, looking back at his past with his searing-never-fading-eyes of the bloodthirsty hunter he had once been. A freefalling arrow he had become which finally, at the end, found its mark in himself. He redeemed himself not for the afterwards world but for an everyday wonder called life.

Sharp city teeth sink into me as I drive back.

A saw cuts through my head. A hacking headache is what I am holding in my hands but then I hold it to the attention of the reading of the psalms and alone comes the Light through those regions of rapture and beats to an end the tumultuous assault as psalm 119 comes to a close and I have a singularly supernatural miracle by 5.30 and I have one hallelujah on my lips and one within me.

Want very badly to succumb to lust's tradition. Desire is straightforward. The clothes Kaia wears give off so much heat that it frustrates the already sweltering weather even more. I am the man in each theme of her extremely adult body. I cannot have a single moment of morality until I have had a prone meeting with her but then she is in a furious solitude but then Deb also takes up bed residency in ours.

New celibacy charges the moments of the morning but I find enough hard masculinity at the thought of the wife who wears so many tight hugs in that dress she wore yesterday that I will need another Christian lifetime to meet them all. For one lifetime, you have to be the world, wedded to a woman. Worry is her new camp. It's about her Focus Academy money. She considers it wasted but as she is very money smart, I make a suggestion: *ask Focus Academy if they will adjust our nephew in place of our son.* She calls them up instantly and it is done. Jonah can have a new beginning from tomorrow. The door on waste is closed. Overjoyed with the news, he exclaims *the doors are opening for me.* He has to visit Hategarh however, for a day.

A civilisation of hate, death, darkness and sadness is an adversary of a good family's love, life, light and laughter. A man called Ram Rahim, lust lord, lord of neon myth palaces, hellhound of nocturnal circuses has a whale's influence on people. He has a long past of wrong doings and now it has all come out into light and long bleeds the country with rat waves of rioting and death and destruction. The NCR is also very, very hunched under section 144. Markets are closed. Roads are closed. Schools are closed. Jonah cannot go beyond the bus terminus.

This is a weekend opportunity for me to make Kaia my captive. After tea, I strip her shoulder since I don't always interact with the clothes. Anyway, they are incapable of holding back my kissing breath and it is quite possible that both of us begin to experience drowned members. *Now you hug me* I tell her and she unleashes love's software and hardware on me wholeheartedly. Diaz, full of life, light, love and laughter, opens conversation with Jonah at breakfast but the latter is a little wary. In the weak hours of the afternoon, Jonah and Dona follow me around like subtitles in the city's old quarter, carrying the groceries. I must admit, I feel multiplied by their strength and while the world is still in the sun, we get home. After all the cooking, I am well-wounded in the greater and the lesser limbs. Jonah rescues them by pressing the lesser and Kaia gets the greater ones off the ground and I take the bed and she puts my feet on and about her and they ride her lap and she also removes their population of nails and restores and rejuvenates them and they forget all the miles they have ever walked and oil is good if it can get home to Kaia's head and Jonah does that for her at the end. Must wait for a star to be added to the night to meet her in their shadows. Short of taking citizenship of her body, I bare edges off her as much as possible in tortured control since Deb is in the same bed. Under the cover of some skins, I don't think there is a human there. But Kaia is forever real.

It is a new dark, every day, into which I wake up at 3.15. Though my face is immersed deep in the night, it puts a smile on my face through to the end besides making the gigantic day, my brother. Thus saith the ink *our darkness is wrenched out of him and the house as the word of God is read out on the audio Bible.* This reading invests into me days of lights even when I turn into a man (I am not one of height) of great length when I hit the sack after work and lunch.

The fiction of real life is uncontrollable. Wife's retail is open. She lets me hold her in my lap and I end up paying love tax by massaging her head. She has a headache and that's because she allows work to follow her home. She asks *how do you do it? You sleep at 1.00 and then get up at 3.30 and then cook? 3.15,* I correct her. Everyone feels how quickly we have taken July to August from last week to this week, yesterday to today, night to morning and then to now. Deb is ordering Jonah to do something.

He says *yes mom* and carries it out. The girl level in her is going down in comparison to the level of mature woman rising.

Kaia oils my hair and says *you should oil your hair. They look like tanned night and you look more predictable.* So I am officially returned to oil after 25 years. Diaz is a brand leader and forgives first and presents Deb with new earphones. Jonah is on an artistic spring and learns fast the tricks of my other trades. He does get my focus. Dona remains the means of our entertainment. The rains and the heat are a temporary arrangement now. Dussehra is at the end of September.

I pursue my needs alone as Kaia gets busy with distempering the house. I have overlooked sleep but I am not overlooked by it and it catches me in school. It's no longer money or marriage. Both have taken a turn. Money is a forgotten mere means. The number of children has gone up. Home has become a competitive place for love and affection, I agree.

We are socially unlimited creatures but there has to be an end. I am unfollowing my FB friends and have not posted anything. Deb's will for music prevails and she makes us listen to Justin Bieber. My body is giving in to the effects of malnutrition. I need daily deliverance from the sin of gluttony among a few more.

Have backup time. Love first. Be creative. Be young. Or do all three: be young, creative and love first or may be look at it in a different order. Love first, be creative and be young. And your mood will never be off and there will be change from anger into something that God has a taste for. He is the coming one, anyway.

11.
Life is not the length of a film

I win a little smudge from Kaia's lipstick on my cheek after fixing her tiffin and seeing her off till the lift. She is working but the day finds a place for the rest of us to be together since it is a holiday today. After breakfast, I visit old Gurgaon with Jonah and Dona. Since dinner matters today, I buy meat, tandoori roti and biryani from whatever shops still have them in the masjid complex. Encounter a lifetime of clouds and rain. Night of steady stars after Kaia has had korma and finds the house very tidy. The thought of going to church next day grows adversely on me as I lie down extremely exhausted by all my toils and she oils my head and my limbs.

The morning's curtains go up on the steam from our tea cups and our fight over Jonah and Dona but God is on our side and with one of His hands, He lifts us and puts us in the church. There is a speaker today and our padre conclusively introduces him with 'he has one wife' and after the high moving words of the visiting sermon, dismisses him with 'if you are addicted to applause, then also I will not applaud you!' The day has a different finish with Kaia being very lovey-dovey in bed.

Deb has made Doe her responsibility. She gives her purple shalwar kurta to her to wear to YWCA teacher's day celebration and directs with her mobile camera, the remaining evening in documenting the unfolding style comedy from the country.

Teacher's day. A day of ambiguous dignity. I decide not to go to school. But my temper is tested and I cross all description of dignity, bellowing at the maid over a mere lost knife. My own salt cannot endure me after that, leave alone of others'. A deepening darkness I feel as everyone comes out to gaze at me. I am a man who faces the psalmist's prayers in the morning and yet I have made the morning suffer. I step out into lost daylight all of a sudden, knowing I'll be missed by Deb who had asked me to drop her. Redemption does not meet me until evening. Jonah, Doe and Deb play hide and seek and the sun sets, adding momentous shadows to their perfect game. When it stops, they surround me, laughing as I analyse Deb's childhood paintings. There is some hope for me in this thing I do, that is, also making people happier. After that moody shadows inspire Jonah to do some sketching and painting. A conference of sunsets. Nature in its first state. Mixing sunsets. A farting cloud. Some other sun themes. Limbo spirits. Naked heaven. Abysmal stars in moonlight dresses. Kaia is in no mood-ambiguity and slams my soul with guilt saying *because of you the maid has left. Now get a new one.*

Distemper and tempers begin. Running away is a good start to cooperating with work which is Diaz's way. *Manage the day without me* he says and leaves fresh-faced. Evening becomes our holiday when he returns

141

fresh-faced and takes us all to Leisure Valley to eat out and we do it best at Royal Restaurant, where the poetry of the past is cast in pictures on wall panels in the dining hall, the size of a palace, and yet the best things of life cannot be photographed.

We are definitely lost with day two of distemper, trying to adjust our own patience against Diaz's lack of it when he returns in the evening and finds no food, the recliner dirty and his watch missing but moderation is achieved when the latter is found later, the furniture cleaned and finally enjoyment of heaven is a happy eternity which begins with ordering pizzas and culminates at McDonald's.

I use tongue temper on day three of distemper when I return from school and the work is still going on and we eat on the bed. I am on better edge however, after some sleep but by this time Kaia's evening is in a white heat. She goes down perhaps to cool it off with a walk. It's late but we seek direction in eating out but she doesn't join us. Diaz tries but fails and leaves her languishing in pain. A kick shows in our step as we run around in Hong Kong Mall to find at least one restaurant open. *Taste of Tamilnadu* is just about to close when we walk in but Deb's expanding countenance shrinks when she learns that they have run out of whatever she selects on the menu and the whole manoeuvre to find happiness loses meaning.

Normal is severed this morning. Our food world is disrupted. Kaia does not prepare the regular course of vegetable and roti but we are compelled to be happy anyway and I boil rice and make dal. On the way back,

I buy sabzee and roti for fibre does feel good with some carbs. Normal is new by the end of the day, however. Jonah is the shaper of this part. He makes chowmein. We party on it and finish it. He makes more and Kaia on her return transitions into extraversion. From the crazy chaos of the tasty noodles finally, a smile is birthed and we have love. She is stirred to talk to him about Dona for whom some monthly money has been created on account of her late mother but who awaits a legal misfortune to befall her unless she has a bank account for its transfer, so Kaia broadens the effort with her experience, style and direct approach and talks to a Babuji in Hategarh while Jonah paces about in the drawing room. She scolds him for trying to act independently and tells him to visit the town next morning with Dona.

News has a kind moment. Jonah has succeeded in getting Dona a bank account. I shift about the mess in the balcony and the study, put up pictures etc, spend time knowing the house and getting tired. A person can become all aching teeth or stomach or heart or head or legs. Kaia is at my feet and takes possession of them in her lap and presses them. I rise again to have a pizza-slice of life which Deb has ordered. She too meets my feet with an infinity of ointment massage. This is a daughter's love. She might not obey instantly and might get angry but her love? *Oh Deb, you are created in the moulds of preteen suede. Your place in our world, your world makes all the difference in all the world to us. You are a socially unlimited edition of endlessness. You have given your will to music and your body to no worry. That you are true every day to whatever is youth. That every time you are angry, we need to change. We need your daily deliverance from pain and stress. By this, you own us because every day we are in pain. You give us the hope of a day called tomorrow because today is a day of reverent love. This is your concept of the future. You know parents are to be treasured. How the other person is feeling is your religion. You don't suffer from the fear of being. Each moment is a normal spark unless amplified by an exploding transparency of very loud expression.* After the massage, I have winged feet. I am picked up on a wind and I go around without the need of any ground beneath me. But there is always the home to fall to after having felt the wind of God and yet I can never walk on water.

Jonah and Dona look like a pair of travelling thoughts, long-travelling through their night, emerging at our door at 6.00 am, a bag for each step on their backs. Clouds have also come like a travelling workforce hence the earth halts today. Holiday is a passing bliss. Deb celebrates her college's golden anniversary by staying at home today.

Kaia has a smile's monopoly on me and so a birthday party follows. Sumer's kid's, to be precise. We drive around asking if there is a birthday celebration in the city. Life is at play at *Café Soul Garden*. The venue is a luxury lot. Fun is catered here in a different way, for example, there are great books on shelves. Among people wearing badges of different ages are young women with a variety of cake-works on their faces. But not the sweet hostess. She welcomes me with her forever kiss. I am a fan friend of that. I know this celebration will be long but the party punch puts Jonah into a negative make at the outset. His long night rises from the sides and surrounds his townships and he lifts his eyes and keeps studying the birthday stars until Sandy grabs a grownup's chance and tries to make him at least quarter happy. We have got around a table and it plays the part that tables play because at the end, we are trying to part and it is difficult and all due to a nephew from Lucknow. He is made up of extraordinary friendly fun. Thanks to him, the salad party is such a success. We invite them to dinner next weekend.

Work leaps from afternoon to evening. Spent a wife while in her arrested embrace. Find time for the Dougs around dinner. Doug aunty brings age to relationships. Sandy is gripped by the greed of watching a match and switches on the plasma and that means ceaseless television of a game that is beyond watching. Our country's massive lengths and breadths are pitched with miles and miles of it and when a day needs us, we give several away. Causing embarrassment is embedded in my style so I order it to be switched off but good is willed by Kaia alone who tells me *it's just a game on the screen* and I say *but you have taught me to dislike TV when guests are around.* Next, his daughter, who is episodes and episodes of flannel from her hair to her eyes to her smile to her voice to her attitude to her gestures to her clothing, gets a feel of fun into a smile and jumps into the empty sofa near my stool while elders are still standing around. That girl gives nothing away! But I have hope that she is designated for love. Driven by evil intent or may be to din into her an episode of propriety, I check her and make her get up. This insane behaviour shocks Kaia and she keeps cornering me about it later. Stone spent by 11.00 pm.

3.15 am. The day awaits me but I reset the alarm. Kaia becomes conscious of me getting back into bed and I get allowed again all the stuff including embraces till the country song of my sinus is interrupted by the second alarm at 4.15.

Jonah picks up some night on his canvas by trying charcoal. I detect traces of fire in Kaia's flower nighty. She is sun's freight today. There's a whole country of new feelings in her experienced embraces.

Sedated by the thought that holidays begin from today and yet managing to see live dawn. Mainstream traffic time since I have to drop Deb off to Huda. Women with extraordinary new designs rushing about.

Dawn decides early earth. After dropping Do and Deb, I have the whole morning to pass in a nursery. Children of overtly earthen build, colour and attire occupy the lift. I have the same attributes and yet I have the effects of a new immortal on them by screaming to get away from my plants. When Kaia's smile voltage goes up, I know she is in a safe mood. After seeing the gardening changes I am making, she remembers the balcony from its lesser days.

In an utterly significant leap, Dussehra and Diwali have moved up into the year. Kaia has hours of emotion after Diaz buys clothes for Jonah from *Lifestyle*. We eat at *Lock-Up*. The place has an iconic, cultic feel. The iron bars. The handcuffs. The ropes. Deb sleeps in the other bedroom but luck remains silent as I am exhausted but my flesh will take a turn in a day or two.

12.

Do coals eventually love the fire?

A white rainy morning that includes church. Jonah shows some young anxiety as he decides which new clothes to get into. A day of envy as Kaia gets to meet and invite her school buddy, Amrita, who exhibits extraordinary psychic superiority. For Kaia, the stars of those days are faint just as all the other stars down the years. For her friend, even the candlelight of those days is as bright and clear as this afternoon sun and yet the latter must not be kept from setting because we are exhausted but only after she leaves. Night's lotus opens up amidst dots of time. The four children keep their laughter active throughout the night in the other bedroom. Way past midnight when the moon is dismissed from the window over me, I tap into my database of desire. The planets are flung aside and I burn into the suns of Kaia's flower nighty. The sky is reset in the pools of human moons, happy like mirrors that will reflect in the light of another day's soon-sun.

The darkness moves aside and in great joy I want and find the morning and the children are also back with their happy noise. Morning is what a good breakfast makes and the spirit children, Jonah and Dona, harnesses their training and talents in making a hearty meal of *aloo ke paranthe*. So when you want happiness you get it. I am obliged to explode a creativity bomb in a white, gold and green blitz of spray-paints. When the atomic air is lost, my craggy POP sculptures achieve a thickening of praise from Jonah. Eve now looks cold as life and the Entity dead as air but he says they are ready for exhibition. The night cannot be twinkly until Diaz has shown us *Hell or High Water*. As the hours go, we step out late but there is more light in an odd hour ice-cream than any. The miracle-handed soul named Deb massages Kaia's back then presses my feet at zero hour.

When the sun reaches the place where it goes away, I get the feel of an addicted wife entering the house looking for me. It is a success, an achievement even though I need many more lives to make my marriage perfect. Anyway, I dive straight out of sleep into the bathroom and begin taking out the washing from the machine but she follows me in and I have to get more of wife by lounging in bed and wrapping her up in a creative massage.

Contentment, simplicity and modesty are what Dona wears. She doesn't even ask for a smile. However, an occasion is given to me to get her some new adornment for a cousin's wedding in *Kasganj*. Even though I say to Jonah, you are worthy of my clothes, he processes and designs his own style by shopping next day on his own. But besides change of fabric, he needs some architectural changes like losing some weight. They return after two days on a common course of guided neon but Jonah still leaves a hair trail in his wake and mystical Dona always dreams as in the wedding pictures.

I catch a corner of the day to go to old Gurgaon with Jonah and Dona. Diaz wants to come along. We exchange messages as we wait for him but finally decide to leave and the messages take a toxic turn and it becomes a hard day of emotions for Jonah when he is dealt a few choice abuses. Love will remain Diaz's focus but Jonah will find his night of redemption only after three months. The holidays have begun. This is a hierarchy of twinkling nights in the nation of lights. Stars will have to wait in their traffic for every dot of light of this festival to pass by. There are places where light will leap from cups brimming with fireworks and empty cups away are places which will be out of light, love, laughter and life. Life is not our invention but we invest in our existence by finding stuff and connecting our lives to it. This is what I do in the balcony and Kaia comes and looks at it and her shine lines of happiness stretch from ear to ear and says *it's like we have a part of a room in a butterfly world.*

Jonah's versatility is tapped by Kaia. She asks him to accompany Deb to the passport office. Heard from aunt Doug that aunt Ida, sister number two of my late mother, has taken the one way turn, folding up into afterlife. She is doing the forever now, taking the adventure forward. The universe is also happy with Dona. Her teachers have praised her performance in the exams.

Life is the writing on the wall. Kaia reads it wrongly. *My new boss*, she cries. Jonah is down with viral and only comes with his eyes to the dinner table. He doesn't speak when Kaia asks him, *how are you feeling?* Deb says *at least speak, she is asking you a question.* He only hardens his scary irises at her. She returns it with her own lengthy look.

Another day of miles for Dona and Jonah. After they leave, we get behind our tongues in arguing over where and when to travel during Christmas and then we cross the dark frontiers of the mind and the soul's planets and that is where I see that I have transformed because I don't budge over my stand that Jonah and Dona will live in the house as long as they need to. From here I see shapes that need to get hunted. I have known darkness that takes unknown forms. Or the unknown takes the darkness we know so that we can be lost in it. But if we know this, we can have confidence that we will find our path because the tongue knows the path it takes. I am told *leave with them and live wherever you want to.* Diaz senses the whale I'm silently trying to overwhelm within me and Deb massages my feet with oil.

13.

Fading flowers in a season of shadows

*D*eep night-side. Trained to feel love. Kaia and I turn from our hate-side and become intensely alive and we plunge into naked sleep. Jonah and Dona return from Hategarh. We feel like lights going to church. Kaia tells Jonah *now Jonah start speaking to Diaz*. Even Rev Cherub is possessed with light today and gives a short, sweet and relevant sermon. From church we make a profane transition to CP where stirred to great laughter, we create so much space of happy moments around us that people have to sidestep us.

Passage-point narrows for Ulysses. It is not a sun generated drift but work generated. My lounger life at school is threatened due to politics over my annual day play. For all the truth I try to bring into my plays, I have been accused of putting layers in it. Hence, I will be ready to readjust to life at school after three days of career fever with loose *emotions*, loose motions and resulting weakness. Deb chooses the heart part by staying at home to take me under her care. I need to be on the side of Light but end up arguing with the tenth floor woman over her mere question *are you the lift repairman?*

The world has its proportion of idiots. That's me with full access to faults. I need a good thousand starts every day to be simply human. But I have insect self-control. Besides, if an insect has done something, I have too in this life. A rage war is what I wage, honking and gesturing at drivers who try to get into my lane as I drive Kaia, Diaz and the three high teenagers to Kashmiri Gate to get MIL's grave work done. That finishes the choice for Diaz to be in a normal state of mind. He always carries his thunder with him and refusing to set foot into the chaotic fullness of Chandni Chowk, takes the metro home. He and Deb are picked from paradise. Not me though. Once we reach Bhagirath Palace, I switch to insect nature and follow Kaia through the insect alleys that burst out at us from every which way. Once you are in the warren, there is no turning back. Keep going back only in your mind if you get lost. From time to time, she stops to perform an insect-check on the stragglers and calls me by my insect name, saying, *hurry up Bug*. This is a sunset city cast in glass of every conceivable colour, shape and size and there is no limit to being original. You could have a dawn there but you wouldn't know without the attendant details. The shop we stop at, Kaia has illuminating moments, finally getting to buy a huge lamp stand and a chandelier. After that an outbreak of dual fun. Eating leftovers at home and then driving with Diaz to Kebab Express at Huda Metro. In the end, we end up putting our mouths into smiles with a good deal of light on the teeth.

Earth's makeup is God-made but the morning gets a new tone in its makeup accidentally from my vaporous paints while painting some of the balcony stuff. The skin of the drawing room gets occasioned in a mist too. It's a crime of colour and the air, floor and water doctors, that is Deb, Dona and Jonah, swing into action and clean the furniture, screen door, floor and carpet with cloth, water and vacuum cleaner. At night, Diaz inspires us with *History of Violence.*

Farmers have been measuring their finished fields by fire and suddenly everyone in the NCR is living in gasping circumstances. My school is airtight but it gets closed too like all others. There is an attempt at surprise but I know that Deb, Jonah and Dona have gone out to purchase cards and what not. You feel loved. It's beginning to look a lot like there's a birthday celebration coming up though there is still time before it will all be candles, cakes and cards. Happiness is such a human thing but my birthday makes me nervous. When we all get to the night, Diaz walks in with a cake and shawarma. It's beautiful what these two children do. The beauty of making a birthday seem like a birthday, is a talent. Love is depicted in their kissing and gifting and cards.

Diaz and Kaia gift me an expensive watch that is the stuff of personality I don't have. A cutting edge rhythm as big as a pendulum. Seized some food at Chillies. One birthday down. The next exhausting one is Jesus's. I am older by a dream today.

Ice night at Kingdom of Dreams. With the childhood changing powers of the wonderland, emerges Alice for all ages, in a body class of her own, moulded in beautiful relief from elaborately white neon or as if from misty polar pools of vanilla ice-cream. She makes you think of a long family history of glorified ice. The memory of her ballet act will erode but every adult will remember her, swimming intimately in shimmering black vodka of the inner mind. I want to be close like those children below in the front rows even though I am incorrigibly on age-battery. And yet I believe in an ever changing existence on an endless scale.

Love is always tested. And contested.

Failure chooses the beautiful. Defeat chooses the brave. There is not a single day of invincibility in our lives. Kaia asks *why are we having this celebration?* She declares that it is a one-sided affair. But we have to do this for the young. They are beautiful and brave. They believe they are invincible. So keep battling the differences. Never question the myth. A perfect end is what we strive for as long as possible. Family is an institution. Complexity is an examination. Commitment is hard work. Love is learnt. And God gives the pass certificate.

He creates a daily night and a daily day so that we could sing a happy long love song. We *have* to celebrate our 25th in a major way.

I thought we would be caught in an early celebration but midnight itself is distracted with all the racket made to wake us up and a tug of hugs and kisses and cards and cakes from the four cousins. Each new blessing has a day but just now it seems it's all crowded into one hour in this heart like house where Deb and Diaz and Jonah and Dona have hearts like houses.

A wedding cake sunrise today. When it is past the hilltops of Aravalli, I post a paean to Kaia on FB, the utopia of wandering faces, and soon the whole world knows. Yea! We made it and the world parties today. The hotel is not as big as our twenty five years but we can get more than just relatives in here. We get closer and closer to compliments as the evening gets younger and younger and are ready to be marked by makeup, that is, foundation and lipsticks rubbing off on us from cheeks and lips rouged with affection and we meet hearts, flowers and gifts with outstretched arms. A few more details of happiness are the silver anniversary balloons Deb has put up on the wall which cut a little colour into the photographs. Kaia is the woman most fantasised tonight. Suddenly, Chitra, Sandy's wife, waves a twinkly hand at us and asks us to speak 'what your marriage has made you'. And as eyes play billiards in their sockets, watching us both, I put on a glib word face and read a part of my paean dismissively while hers are the best of the caught heart-moments. Sadness has been waiting in the corners of her mouth and eyes and it makes her speech wind up in her throat with a choke over the words *my sister couldn't come*. Unlike her, I have never tried to find if there's a serious moment in my life. I cannot ever place the satire aside. How else can we best analyse the world? She makes a soul movement by acknowledging that she has four children. That makes her better of the best women. We try to understand Diaz's friends in the light of their smiles at all his jibes at their expense. Deb is also friend-flavoured with Padhiri who has all the ingredients that takes to make a girl. The function had started as a shadow with silhouettes of wind around the piano in some inactive background but when Simeon touches the keys, light rushes to the drought dew, now falling in shapes of sound. He is representing Dididi's family. Ladies accumulate around him and sing hymns till the end. Life is such a precious attachment but goodbyes grow upon the late hour. We emerge like new brood of light from the foyer and fill the night with meaningful laughter and the car with the love gifts and balloons. We pursue the road home but there is nowhere like a happy tomorrow until tonight is fully consumed, that is, all the gifts have been opened, all the talk is done, all the relatives discussed and all of Kaia I have had. She sits in bed, reading my paean but I don't allow her to waste more time and pull her to me. The night is a fresh bedsheet, washed with moonlight soap, under the new counterpane gifted by Jonah and Dona and the best way to be the moon is to go up and stay close and not interrupt. We put the dawn away and sleep in consensual naked ink.

I have reached a heart's milestone. Whatever that is. Like a peace seeking wanderer, looking for his metamorphosis, Jonah follows Simeon to Jolly Grant in the morning. The anniversary balloons make the wall something else.

The winged week that created and threw into itself both my birthday and our wedding anniversary is gone.

14.

Traces of space

I have a series of lives to live, including keeping up with Kaia because her mind is a raging storm as Dona, Deb and Diaz force her to take them to The Air Force Auditorium. We assure her that we are party-trained. Trusting us on that, she steps into the main lines being the anchor for her company's Customer Day and we step into the side lines of a table beneath a fire and adapting to starters and juices. She is in her social silk and when the time comes to begin, uses her voice by occasion. I am invited to the bottle but cannot indulge being the official family chauffeur. We are given to protein-slavery but don't mind finding a fried vegetable now and then because we suffer from meal-stupidity and would have better capacity to eat with Kaia but find ourselves in a kind of eating pain which can only be relieved by visiting the washroom where already men are lined up, peeing from the door. It's very difficult to even get in but I find it acceptable to perish there, purging body's godzillas, than on the road.

Morning is a pencil shaded, dull fluid light on Jonah's canvas when he returns with gifts from Dehradun. *He will be weighed by his heart* says Kaia for the nice keychain he has given her. As gold has a creed of its own,

I present my fat gold ring to Kaia as a gift. A rain sunset grows upon the peace balcony, now a combination of work, art, plants and lights. I have involved hues from different sources during the day and a measure of lights I have bought for the night; for true light who can afford and maintain? But if I have it, how much more easy it would be to keep the steady darkness beyond the plants' periphery!

Jonah and Dona have had a good Christmas upbringing in Hategarh and decorate the drawing room very imaginatively. Happiness spreads its lace across Kaia's face.

I have a smile opposite tonight as four days of annual day madness get over. Everyone including the principal liked the play. Certainly, miracles don't make a noise and I return in silent jubilation and pass under a sparkle or two from the twelfth floor balcony in all its jazz details. Seems like we have stars for life. Their light cannot be recalled in the morning.

I am in the vicinity of a choice and say a surprising yes to Kaia asking about church. There is visible love in her mouth, shaping itself into a kiss for me but she will be heartbroken as the sin of pride is always staring at me. The body and spirit alarms of holiness do not warn me about the impending fight with the parking fellows after the service. I will be well-wounded by its memory for some time.

We rise out of the night like beings of the beginning with our hearts' lights ready for the road. There is a light's Godzilla at the end, that is, the gravitational sun.

It also rises towards our flight and Kaia and Diaz are put through a smile and there is a pause in my silvering and for Deb there is some apocalyptic mythologizing art in the clouds. We make a new start from Kochi airport because now there is a road and a cover of light over everything from mostly Mary's pictures and statues but after several hours, when we have gone beyond the edge of meaning, Deb asks *where have you people taken the hotel?* The answer she should get is: It's the hotel which has taken us and so at last after several more hours we enter the freedom land of shadows. A chugging ferry fetches us over a dark river sparkling with a thousand winks. Here, limbo itself is wasted. Here the end rises to meet us. What will we need here? Here are the ancestors of vegetation. Fathers and mothers of flora. In a wandering multi-headed light, are swarms of bathing ducks and an equal number in the green producing grass and climbers and creepers and trees and palms, stretching perhaps from the beginning of the sun to the end of stars. We are met by a balding father of smiles at the hotel. *Take days* he says *but end your mind here and start your heart and soul. Whatever you have known life to be, whatever your experience of the world, changes here.* His staff are light turners too, a little different at different times of the day. At night, they are broadest like lightning from which they can wrench a thunder and put it in your bosom. They are the beings of the beginning.

Our love, light, life and laughter become those of fools because by lunch a hole has worked itself into these and caused a fight over Jonah and Dona who are not even with us. We give ourselves a gap through a long nap. At its end, we find a sunset. Kaia and I are awake in its faceless, bodiless, nameless ink. It erases our Adam and Eve and we sit like cramped fairies outside. In the quit light from the far houses across the river, gradually, we are able to discern part of a smile of one member of the hotel staff. Before he leaves or his smile, we order room service for Diaz and Deb and coffee for us. The weather's breath is in our faces and lapping at our feet is a denseness that promises no earth at sunrise. This peaceful nothingness over the next course of an hour or two begins to experience a slow avoidance of silence. It is a temple song and music that fills the inflating night with the loneliness of at least a third of angels. Good and bad do get created here, I have a feeling. We are happiness rebels and the closed room makes it possible for love's light and life's laughter to be involved with each other. After the bonhomie, Kaia falls into bed like discarded clothing. We three venture out. Except the stars atop the coconut tree, summer miles for eons have conjured night zones all around, interspersed with mushrooms of Christmas lights. Night may not be a completely passing blank around us but we feel encompassed by a themelessness, set totally against our light, love, laughter and life. Afraid to take a further step into, perhaps, a missing earth, we stare at our returning breath. Taking cue, we go back to the safety of the room. I see blank dreams and keep waking up between them. There is no sound. Not even barking. This land can be written about but not interpreted.

There is no movement but we keep approaching somewhere until, at the concurrence of night's end and sleep, an amorphous dawn scratches at the surface of my sleep buried soul. There is an order of light against the appearance of the sun anywhere. In the labouring rays, the rich iconography hangs in casual meditation. Flowers present an action to my word butterflies. There is a snakebird at sky's ease in the tallest coconut tree. I perceive some more sunrise in the greater skin of the biggest and fattest caterpillar, anyone has ever seen, on our steps. The owner comes out of nowhere and deposits it in a hedge where it wags in my face like a shy first finger. At worst are the convulsive predatory birds. I want to lounge in the sunrise but much darkness is still on the grass and I run into a rash of itching mosquitos. I cannot go back to the room. Profane wind silhouettes have accumulated around me and make my body all music. A cloud seems to grow over the whole place then shrinks as a rushing light breaks out over the reclusive lilies in full bloom-communion with the waves under their broad leaves. After breakfast, we make Godzilla's rush to the swimming pool. This is the fish way to be happy in this version of the real fish waters. The race we get in the limbs is like what stones get from a slingshot. We are united by laughter with the sun which we squeeze out of our swimming costumes but not from our skins. I so badly want to squeeze out Kaia from her costume. Oh, the way water has with some women; I can never tire of them. She further ripens herself into a waxy drowsiness with a full-body massage. Deb joins her. Three women, slow smile spirits in pulp art fashion, appear outside our door to clean the room when we are leaving to tour the city. Our own smiles are in parts for everyone from the manager to the always waiting boatman. Throughout the day, the sun burns to be the night. When we return, the long road is a narrow trail of the long gone sunset so we have to get behind the half hair headlights that fail to inflate the blankness. Earth is missing all around and all along. The boat is waiting against the order of light not to be here all by itself. Its light labours through darkness' other layers to take us back to our room. We ask the monopoliser of smiles to serve us coffee, green tea, fruit salad and sleep. Kaia's swimming costume, gathering the night in the veranda, is in the way of my midnight.

I feel new, unwound from my dreams but immortality is only in bees' hearing but they aren't here. I return to the room and start the pen after my quest for tea is fulfilled. Earth is still in light ink. Way past a lot of pen and ink, Diaz gets up and sits with a dreaming expression and life is a living memory and I know it when I see him eating leftover fish and prawns from last night's dinner. These memories I have wanted and I am living the moment of each. We have the chance to grow up in a day like Jo did when his year began but my son and I prefer to grow up with each meal though our entire lives. At breakfast, I cannot take my eyes off the women tourists. Outside some faces, the flower *is* the rose and some bodies are slushed by sky's every sun's heat. A day is never repeated in spite of every day's repetitions of the sun, the wind, the rains, the stars, the flowers, the light, the laughter, the love and the life. The man with the waiting expression is the boatman. He will take us to our driver who will take us to Arundhati Roy's rivers and canals where a side saint will give us tender coconuts and in the waters of the bird sanctuary, there will be intangible birds whom Diaz will only try to catch and the driver will become our friend and eat with us and then there will be the long road where we will ask for light and that will bring us back to the boatman, his waiting expression tangled in watery darkness and we will be led to the room in the light of the boy's smile. He brings us our room service. He is as quiet as the increasing lights of his smiles.

The first finger of the sun dipped in its sunlight, touches my eyes. I step out and have to wait for deeper light for the darkness of the body to depart. Whether the sun is visible or not beyond the coconut tops which seem closer now, deeper light is still the name. The brain is early today so I must return to have my day's fuel of words. Diaz comes and begins perpetuating last night's dinner beside me. That song across the river has timeless existence but it is careful not wearing out the entire mythology. We are on holiday for more life, laughter, light and love. The best of everything is these four. They not only bond with each other, they become each other. We are in the deep part of the day. It is just like woman, dividing where it is deep. There are swamps on both sides. The long trail, with pockets of love and light like the old couple we buy water etc. from, turns into scissors, dividing us up emotionally and physically. As the day's fires close in around us on either side, I feel heavy as a hobbit with dinosaur joints. It is the end of the verbal world for Deb. She is so totally wound down. Diaz is carrying his finer kilograms, poking fun at Deb with his songs from his side. Within minimum visible distance is Kaia. She looks back with a smile. It is the shade we reach ultimately. The Basilica is like God's fireplace. A small school girl is sitting in a corner, seeking warmth but I think it went cold long ago. Out driver Suman brings us a smile in his shining moonlight beard. Though his eyes lack a sunrise, he can make us laugh with mystic abundance. He takes us to places peaking with butterflies but when some begin to show shadows in their parts, we take the long road back. Dissolved in the dimming of Christmas stars are the peace and goodwill carollers in trucks ahead of us. Reindeers aren't tropical but if they are around here, they mustn't be red-nosed. It's now a tradition to meet the twilight and in it are the waiting boat, the hotel and silence. Everything is like a huge painting but you can't gather the painting now can you? And my writing is not the size of life. I pack the bags with whatever we have to take.

A strand of early morning light pierces through. I have decided to venture into those parts where the exotic plants are in the assembly of wind and water in the day not so deep so I put a long walk on the flaky white seashells that stick out on the trail to take away some of them from the root of their dewy dawn. My family can never tire of rest but today they have no option but to embrace the day. Like flexible snails we hurry for breakfast. Suman shows up with his smiling teeth and takes us to the beach and then we add a long party that is not repetitive until it is time to, for the sky to take us home. Much of the night is already there with glowing Christmas makeup on the door and inside everywhere but by the time we reach, undercurrents of the morning are ready to pass with us into the house. There are candles of psychic choosing too and in the ensuing peace and goodwill thereof, we have some lovely korma. Jonah and Dona have tried their best to ensure that God reaches us this Yuletide.

Yesterday's doors close on today, finishing off the career of a few smiles. The unpacking, cleaning, washing, tidying up revives us with exhaustion and all our faces are in fits but Diaz's six-limbed build belongs in a gym. I ask him as he waits for the lift *but didn't you want to help me bake cakes?* Silence explores his face for an answer but there is none. The reason is my hard partner. Kaia has already called him selfish. I imagine we too would love to lick a butterfly but for bees, work is work. Among the plants I have brought is a water lily, a soul plant that will need self-searching depths very quickly and its opposite, the water hyacinth. The inflated costumes of greenness need to float too. In the evening, we are ready with our sun sent faces to fill ourselves with Doug's carol singing and the festival's fillings. We return, each one an architect of singing smiles except Diaz. Tonight, he is not the channel of cheer.

Christmas is inseparable from darkness this morning. And it's not the season thing. There is darkness upon darkness. I drive very fast but mood overtakes us to church. Diaz looks as fresh as vinegar in his drab brown clothes of yesterday. He is facially inches from us at the service but far away from even the Holy Communion with that Greek sculpture's gaze he has begun to get. He takes lunch in the deteriorating lights of the afternoon in which I am laughing and joking with Dona and Jonah. Kaia is doing many hives' work all alone; shifting furniture, tidying, cleaning, dusting. Her mood is off so we can't even dodge the dust. In bed, I should expect intense moments of moonlight but lightening crosses my mind when I turn. Kaia's eyes, in her infinitely transparent face, are piercing the intensely and infinitely nocturnal night. This is going to be my some sort of midnight trial. God-voiced, she asks me *have you spoken to Diaz?* In spite of my self-defence, she wants me to admit my crime that I am involved more with *those two*.

I waste no time in accepting Dididi's invitation to visit her for a higher earth and longer day because the non-hemispheric midnight over here is going to linger around for some time. For our galaxies of life, light, life and laughter, space is required; the kind my Dididi possesses. My goodbye is a monologue. I can comprehend the shadows in the shadow of the tears Kaia is sitting in. Diaz is sowing silence in the other bedroom. My goodbye follows us to the station and now I am enjoying sipping tea at this habitual embodiment of beyond before the bus catches us. I am looking forward to another delightful chance to be different.

When night picks up speed, I wake up. The Volvo is on a slamming rash and reckless, thriller run until what I sense is a motion of colour outside. The sun is at some invisible dawn number on our dials as we disembark at the bus stand at Dehradun and are hammered down by a cold Godzilla's fist. The auto driver is a compiled creature of shawls, caps, face covers, mufflers, gloves etc. One of mankind's original, he is the father of unmanned children. Except his death wheel grip, everything else, including the road, rebels. For an hour or so, echoes of a thin chilling music from a jungle alongside, connect my ears from inside. We are reconciled to the planet only when we reach Jolly Grant. The air changes shape into an outline of houses on both sides of the smooth road of Jolly Grant. Here Jonah joins the fellowship of the route by guiding the auto into lane number 4. Recognition is a gateway and Moldu whimpers since he can tell we all own each other's blood. The iron-gate opens and we walk into a twilight of previous night's embers and pre-dawn eyes. Sully in a tie with his love, is so grounded.

Simeon maintains an ascetic aloofness. Sana is holding her little girl in two of her many arms. I can tell that this place has a history of fairies. A fortress of flowers, many are the gates to this place. Then in the mists of faces we are led inside to my Dididi. Everything here is woven into woman's quintessence of a warm cosy house. Home can never be a mistake in such hands. Our faces peak with love. I lift her up as she calls me '*professor*'. To me, she will always be a candle from the past. After tea, she puts us to bed and lowers the lights to that of our skins. Then a proliferation of senses with ancestral snoring for some time and then very faintly, under the legends of sleep. I wake up into the hustle and bustle of bright sunlight, the one I knew in childhood and it is like I am in a hallucination lane because everything is almost the same: the house and its courtyards in fulltime colour; the orchestral start of bird symphony from tree to tree and the breakfast in the courtyard years ago. It is old home. It always knows the way to the child in you. The little child, Shira, goes around like a little language hawker among a population of rich smiles. Moldu is competing with her with his lone dog show. Later he joins me on a new watch on the roof where I am floating in a swoon. No one makes any sound in the house because they are all trying the day at Sahastra Dhara. Below me Dididi is looking at her inventory of work in this idea called new house. Oh, how she is committed to aesthetic, intellectual and spiritual evolution. Happy wedding anniversary to her and Sully! The far off city day is passing by us very slowly. As far as I can see, people are busy in erasing previous day's dirt from their lives. No one is in a hurry to get to their futures. As the day gets oxidized into evening, the house catches light from Dididi and Sully's anniversary excitement. Even the tranquil artificial flowers notice awhile and comprehend the nature of this millennial event and succeed in looking really lush, luxuriant and fertile. It will always be the other moon's first world on such a night as this. Our hearts are winds of light and love and laughter and life after the lovely dinner from both and Jonah, Dona, Moldu, Deb, Simeon lift us to the terrace where the stars find a route to our laughter etc. The night makes noises around us, trying to understand what this is all about. We come down to a blooming bonfire and form a circle around this further sparkler of what this is all about. The cold night gets going and the fire gets going and the fresh fuel supply gets going and when we have had enough, we get going to our different rooms.

Night is not permanent and morning isn't an option and so is tea. The sun pauses and hours grow old over this mother of all teacups in my hand. Cups as these will always have tea. Then more hours hang over three courses of breakfast which the fascinating Dididi serves us. It is incredible not to think around love and its three other fellows now. In her hands, less grows into more. I have a talent for toil and it is nobler than idleness so I get up and dig up a neglected corner of the courtyard; rearrange some of the potted plants and the world is even more new and I feel there is more of home to have if you have something to do in it always. I would have done more but without the desired greater strength of a young person, I give up. The toil gets straight to the bones. The day's great snail takes away Sully and Jonah and Dona on a visit to some pastor's house. I while away solitude against the sky for hours, thinking of nothing, until the day is on candlelight. The hill is the thought. Birds wind-walk the ground, full of crumbs from the spent day. What a time-lounger I have become in two days. I finally get up. A lot of sun has shined on me and given me an extra tan attachment. Here you can choose the darkness you want. We choose to sing Silent Night today. It is in parts and Jonah loves *What Child is This* calling it *What is This Child*! Leftovers from last night are the great simplifiers of life and tonight's dinner. Jonah, Dona, Deb, Simeon and I walk like a pageant of shadows to fetch a few things from the local market. The moon is in the dew. Moldu has been moving his bit of love around but finally settles on Deb as his bitch. Dididi reclines on the sofa watching television people. We become strong like the age-old songs which we sing until it is time. Our prayers include the seven young futures. A mountain grows in me but an ocean rises in Sully who engulfs my mountain in his embrace and kisses. A universe made of clear moonlight guides us to the terminus. A returning truth fills the human hole in me as we sit in a restaurant, sipping some tea. Someone's everyday life becomes a two-day wonder in someone else's life. What a life that must be! I have to work on making my life to be a wonder for me every day.

It is a sunrise and even though the streetlights and headlights illuminate the Capital city, marooned in dust and ash, busting the century's lungs, I must spend every moment and every chance to allow self-discovery. God makes early mornings. Kaia, my heartbreak half, is the only part that is part freshness, opens the doors to it. I am sitting accepting its rays. Deb, Jonah and Dona's eyes are wasted with sleep and go to their beds. Kaia motions me to also go to bed. In great simplicity of obedience I am a walking smile behind and pass by Diaz, sitting up in his bed and he looks up at me and I touch his face. O how I want to place at least a candlelight in those eyes. The air remains cool and dry for most of the day but there is a floral change to the evening when Kaia returns loaded with bouquets. They are for her mother's first death anniversary so the evening returns to being monochromatic and for some colour, I spend the dots of time in the peace balcony with its fake fairy and revolving lights. The beyond night is still giving stars to those who don't have these.

Kaia's mood helps part time into day and night. In the day I escape from her with a century of smiles where I can think of the edge of the water in Kanji Padam and on the hill in Dehradun. They are there, the stuff of water and the stuff of mountains, when the world first started and the first people roamed those and traversed those and sailed those. But the night is an island and I am alone on it and when the moon is back in the window, I see that it is a vastness which lies against my woman. She is holding another woman who is old and dying and in stages of gently purging sanity until there is nothing but a profound blankness. I see they are inseparable but because of my cruel upbringings, I make it possible. Shakespeare has already run this through his song of seven ages. Loneliness is the final stage but who is the enemy who makes one abandon her mother? Now when I am in bed beside her, she justly turns and addresses me *what about those two? How long will they stay in my house?* I postpone a groan and the night becomes loud between us as we levy accusations and yet the inner woman takes over and passes over to my side and lets me find an embrace. Now the whole thing has been consumed and laid to the end so I wait within as I place the whole situation of '*those two*' in God's hands. I don't have to see it but it is there. At the end of the despair road is a constantly moving horizon talking to a very stable heaven.

15.

Love takes the hurt out of the end

The week's great darkness has flowed from the core of Xmas till New Year's Day. We have not received any light from Diaz's eyes. We are so used to him being the moment and not this silent gallery of gloom in all the pictures that Deb keeps taking. Under the overhanging noon in Galleria, we are on one bench. He is on another in the shadow of his own fury. There can be no hurried approach to this. Kaia comes out of the bank and according to the last investment in a conversation with him, he refuses to eat with us. I commit this division of love, light, laughter and life into God's hands and wait within. A new world pauses in the depths I have created for the soul and the surface plants and have reserved a reflection for myself at least once in the day in their new place outside the study. The sun does not refuse to peer into it. I cannot say how the moon responds to it but I am completely at home here, starting new murky depths in the middle of the day. Movement of thought is possible only when truth is deep. Preparations have been made for a midnight celebration but the skies are down and the brooding family of life, love, light and laughter must simply crumble into their beds tonight.

The birthday of the young is a ritual of growth so let me try to create an approach to my son through a kiss and a wish on his birthday. He must hurry from his loneliness today. At least he asks me in the morning if I would like some egg. Kaia and he have work but the rest of us run silence or explore the tropics of the mind to find the cause as we go and shop for the celebration. Around midnight, Deb, like a blessing from the book of the young, lays the table but he does not join our smiles so we take the birthday song to him but now the obstacle is the toilet door behind which is the place of his choosing so we sing it there. Finally, he steps into the study and the team of laughter, love, light and life is a still image of defeat but Kaia alone can be a storm of light, love, laughter and life and she owns the words of these so first she arms Dona and sends her into the study, followed by Deb, followed by Jonah, followed by herself, standing in the doorway. I remain a companion of the candles on the silent cake, now beginning to have a future in wax melting on cream. Kaia's gusts end and my son's smile is set at liberty and in the wake of it, ours follow their destinations too and with smiles singing, the candles are blown out, the waxed cake is cut and happy birthday is chanted once again. Kaia sighs great relief as the multi-member of the family is back, declaring *I was laughing all the time.* A sun later is Deb's birthday.

Tonight the moon joins us in her midnight birthday celebration.

Peace generation, world girl, Deb is all fine in the sun. Rapturous like a half-angel with two thousand rupees from me to spend in the city with her friend Padhiri, who is a passing bliss on sun's side, who is light as humour, who is transparent as glass extracted from moonlight and who creates a welcome birthday scene in her car for Deb with balloons and banner and so Deb returns a whole soul and puts it to good use on Kaia since she is in, not altogether, some separate sorrow, perhaps beset by family and with a separate heart she joins us, when forced by Deb, to eat the leftover cake and other stuff after which Deb uses her new polaroid, a gift from Diaz. He says glibly *you two get a pic clicked before you get a divorce* to which I add *not yet* and then we all pose and the pics hold a little more than the extraordinary smiles we are giving, except Kaia. For long she sits on the sofa, the deep dew of the eyes hide a rainfall. Deb urges her to name it and she says *I am ready for the divorce* and everyone's face goes into pale time, with soot effect in the eyes, while colour is still developing in the Polaroid pics. I take a separate squeeze of the whole thing and can't help but grin and also shed some unseen but fun tears in the recliner. As a passing essence, she leaves the room while I slip into the peace balcony. Embedded in clothes and shawls, I see the wintry night as only a tepid light dark picture beyond the plants' periphery. Deb plays the peace player and tries to call me out of the conference of lights but then out of darkness' own perfect reality, comes forth the wife and forcing her way into the peace balcony, takes me to bed and we sleep with a sense of repaired doom. She has a death-control over me. Neither can I let go of her. The end is, therefore, refusing to come because I am on life terms with the four members of this marriage: Life, Love, Light and Laughter. We are watching *Aftermath*.

I hear heavenly popcorn popping like parts of a heavenly laugh.